Marcus Sedgwick
FLOODLAND

Wood engravings by the author

Orion
Children's Books

First published in Great Britain in 2000
as a Dolphin Paperback
Reissued 2005 by Dolphin paperbacks
Reissued 2010 by Orion Children's Books
a division of the Orion Publishing Group Ltd
Orion House
5 Upper St Martin's Lane
London WC2H 9EA
An Hachette UK company

 7 9 8

A catalogue record for this book is available
from the British Library.

ISBN 978 1 85881 763 7

Typeset at The Spartan Press Ltd,
Lymington, Hants

Printed in Great Britain by
Clays Ltd, St Ives plc

The Orion Publishing Group's policy is to use papers that
are natural, renewable and recyclable products and made
from wood grown in sustainable forests. The logging and
manufacturing processes are expected to conform to the
environmental regulations of the country of origin.

www.orionbooks.co.uk

For Kate

before

 one

Zoe ran. Harder than she had ever run in her life. Her feet pounded through the deserted streets of derelict buildings. Somewhere, not far behind, she could hear the gang coming after her. It felt as if her heart would burst, but she didn't slow down. She'd been planning to leave the island for a long time, but had been putting it off. It was a big decision to set out to sea in a tiny rowing boat. Now she had no choice.

Before, no one had bothered her. Zoe was a loner. Most of the people left on Norwich hung around together in groups, but she preferred to be on her own. It was safer that way, because you never knew whom you could trust.

Somehow, someone had found out about the boat she'd been hiding. A boat was an escape route, a way to get away from Norwich, which got smaller every year, as the sea kept on rising. It didn't matter that there could only be room for two people at most in her boat. Others had joined in the chase, and now a mob of about fifteen people was hot on her heels. There was only one way out; to get to her boat before they got to her. So she ran on, while her body screamed for her to stop.

"Get back here!" someone yelled angrily at her, though they couldn't see her.

It wasn't far to the little shed where she'd hidden *Lyca*, her boat. A couple more streets of derelict shops to where what was left of the city fell away into the sea. If the sea hadn't come she might have been shopping here herself, with her parents perhaps. From much practice she squashed the thought of her parents as soon as it started, and kept on running.

Just before she rounded a corner, she heard more shouts from behind. They had seen her.

"There!"

"Come on!" shouted another voice. "Get her!"

Scared, she made the corner, but her feet slipped from under her on the wet ground. She went sprawling, and slid clumsily in the mud. She started to panic badly, and made a mess of getting up again. She had dropped her pack as she fell, but there was no time to pick it up.

The sound of running feet came closer. Another two seconds and they would be round the corner. She got up and practically threw herself over a wall. She landed awkwardly, but she'd won a little more time. She was in a graveyard. It led away down a hill to where a small brick shed stood near the water's edge. Once it had contained all the equipment for looking after the graveyard, but now it contained Zoe's boat. The previous night she had rowed around from the warehouse where she had found the boat and fixed it. The old building had been unsafe when she'd discovered it, and had been getting worse. She had decided to find a new place to keep her boat, and the shed seemed ideal.

In the dark she had dragged the boat the short distance from the water to the shed. It had been very hard work. At night she hadn't noticed the deep ruts the boat's keel had made in the sodden grass. In daylight, even in her mad rush, they were obvious. She would be lucky if no one had already found it.

"*Lyca*," Zoe panted as she opened the shed door, "please be here, *Lyca*."

It was all right. The boat was still there waiting for her.

Pulling it across the grass, and then into the water, she dared to look behind her for the first time. Her stomach twisted with fear. The gang were storming down the hill, weaving in and out of the crumbling gravestones. Zoe moved faster. She clambered aboard and put the oars out, then started to pull. They were at the water now, and though one or two stopped, the rest came splashing madly after her.

"Take me with you!"

"Come back! We won't hurt you. Just take us with you!"

Zoe could see their eyes, clearly. She saw fear. But she couldn't trust them. Since she'd lost her parents, she'd made it a rule not to trust anyone. Zoe had heard people say they'd lost someone, when really they meant they had died. In Zoe's case, 'lost' meant exactly that. It was still unbelievable, and so stupid.

She looked at the crowd in the water again. If she went back, there'd be a fight over her boat, and she wouldn't get a look in. She rowed on, pulling harder, even though she was safely away.

Slowly, she watched as the people dragged themselves out of the water and waded back to the shore. Natasha was there too. That hurt most of all. Natasha was the closest thing she had to a friend. Zoe used to see her when the supply ships came, before they stopped coming. After that she saw her sometimes at the allotments, when she went to put some work in to earn food. They would only have a little chat, but it was enough to keep Zoe from cracking up. But now the allotments had sunk into chaos, too.

Zoe suddenly remembered their conversation the last time they'd met. She had been about to tell Natasha about her boat, and her plans to escape, but had decided not to. Maybe Natasha had guessed? From something Zoe had let slip? It didn't matter now. The crowd stood quietly, watching her as she rowed away.

Zoe didn't feel scared of them any more.

"Sorry," she said to herself, quietly. She began to cry, but she didn't stop rowing. Her uncut hair fell across her eyes, but she didn't stop to push it away. Still she rowed on, her thin hunched frame working the oars until finally she had to pause for breath.

Feeling around in her pocket she fished out her compass. It was the last thing she owned that had belonged to her parents. For that reason she'd kept it in a pocket. If she hadn't she'd have lost it when she dropped her pack. It was a little dented from her leap over the cemetery wall, but it was still working.

She pointed herself south-west, and rowed. She couldn't remember the name of the place the supply ship used to come from, but she knew the big bit of Britain was somewhere in that direction.

She was rowing away from all she had ever known. It was a strange thing. Before the previous night, she had only ever pretended to row. Her dad had taught her, in the same methodical way he did everything.

"You'll need to know how to do this one day," he told her.

He'd taught her how to use the compass, as well as a lot of stuff about survival. Just in case the time came when she was on her own.

And so every now and then, when they weren't busy just trying to get by, they'd sit in an old bathtub and pretend to row.

Even though it had seemed like a game to Zoe at the time, he'd made sure she was doing it right anyway. And she knew just how to do it, the only thing that surprised her was how hard it was to pull the oars through the water.

"Why don't you look where you're going?" she'd asked her dad.

"When you're rowing, you mean?" he said.

"Yes. Why do you sit looking backwards?"

"It's just the way it's done," he said. "You couldn't row half as well facing forwards."

It had always seemed strange to her, but now it was even worse. There before her was Norwich getting smaller and smaller with each stroke. She was heading into the unknown, without even looking where she was going.

She rowed and rowed, until her small supply of food had gone. She had put the compass on the floor of the boat in front of her, and every few seconds she checked her direction against it. There was no sign of land now, and a creeping fear began to seep into her. She looked at the compass almost every stroke; it was her only chance now. Like magic, its tiny hand kept pointing in the same direction. It knew where she was going, even if she didn't. She lost all sense of time. The sun was somewhere way overhead, and beat on the back of her neck, making her feel dizzy. She pushed her hair out of her eyes, but the sea wind blew it back across her face. She felt faint. She was in trouble. She had just enough awareness to pull in her oars. Then she slumped over them.

In her stupor she replayed the nightmare where she had lost her parents.

two

After the water came, Zoe and her parents had tried for years to stick it out on Norwich, along with another hundred or so. After a while, they realized they were fighting a losing battle, and that the sea was not going to stop rising. Zoe's mum was ill, too. She seemed to have a sickness that came and went, and had lasted for weeks. They'd had enough.

Back then, there were still fairly regular supply trips from the mainland. A big ship used to bring as much food as could be spared, and anchor half a mile offshore. After rowing in with the supplies and sharing them out, the captain would ask if anyone wanted to leave. Usually there would be one or two more people ready to go to the mainland.

But just when Zoe's parents had decided to get off the island, the boat stopped coming. Instead of the usual four or six weeks, three months went by before it reappeared. Finally it slipped into view late one night, as if the captain knew there would be trouble. By now a lot more people than usual wanted to get off the island. There was confusion; it was dark, and a terrible fight broke out to get aboard the two tiny rowing boats. Zoe helped her dad to get her mum on board one of the boats, just as it was pulling away from the shore. It was already dangerously overloaded. Two men were trying to push each other out of the boat, even as the oarsman took his first strokes. One of them succeeded in shoving the other out. There was only enough time and room for Zoe, or her dad, to jump in.

She saw her dad hesitate. She had never seen that before; he always seemed to know what to do. She could see him torn between getting in the boat with his sick wife, or putting his daughter in with her.

Zoe looked at the other boat; there was still a little room to be had. She decided to help her dad; to make the decision for him.

"You go with Mum; she needs you," she yelled.

"No!" said her dad.

"I'll get in the other one." She pointed. "I'll see you on board the ship."

"No," he said, "You get in the boat . . ."

Then the oarsman noticed them.

"Only one of you!" he shouted. "And make it quick! The ship's already full! We're leaving."

He started to pull hard now.

"Dad! It's only as far as the ship. I'll see you there . . ."

Still he hesitated. Zoe forced her decision. She backed away from the boat.

"I'm going for the other one. Get on board, Dad! Quick!"

She saw the relief in her dad's face as he climbed aboard from waist-deep water.

"Zoe . . . well, go then!" he shouted. "Get in the other boat! Hurry, Zoe!"

Zoe turned and saw with horror that the other boat was already leaving. More people were arriving from the town, too, sensing this could be the last chance to get away. They headed for the boat Zoe was making for. She ran across the slimy muddy shore, and tried to climb in over the stern of the boat, then someone hit her on the chin. She fell back dazed in the mud, and watched as the boats moved away towards the lights of the ship.

Suddenly she realized that she was being left behind. Her dad thought she was on the second rowing boat, that he would see her on the ship. She knew the captain wouldn't come back for her. With all these people there would only be another fight. She had to let her dad know now, before the rowing boats reached the ship. She tried to shout, but her voice was weak with exhaustion.

Then she thought she heard her dad call to her.

"Zoe? Are you there?" came his voice through the dark.

"Dad! I'm here! Come back! Get them to come back! Please!"

She thought she was yelling, but in reality she could only manage a whisper. There and then a numbness came to her. Her brain closed in on itself, blocking out the full impact of what had happened. She blacked out, the sea lapping at her legs.

That was a long time ago, though she had no idea whether it was six months, or even a year. It was impossible to tell. She hadn't thought to mark the days, and the weather was so weird you couldn't even be sure what season it was. After waiting a long time for her parents to come looking for her, she began to lose hope. There was no way off and the supply ship never came again. She guessed life was getting harder even on the mainland. She had been sure her parents would come and find her, but maybe they couldn't get a boat, or maybe they'd never even . . . She pushed that idea from her mind, as always, but it didn't change the fact that she was stuck.

Then she had found the boat.

She rowed and rowed, getting weaker all the time, until finally she collapsed over the oars, exhausted.

The boat drifted.

When she woke, it was dawn.

"Damn!" she yelled, for the whole wide sea to hear. Once again she fought to stop the panic rising inside.

"I could be anywhere."

She checked the compass, against the direction she was drifting in.

"South-west. Could be worse."

Even so, there was no sign of any land, in any direction. But then, turning on the thwart, she saw it for the first time. She opened her mouth in surprise, but said nothing. Far away on the horizon was a massive, ancient, stone building. It had two tall towers that stuck into the sky, one at the end and another shorter one in the middle. She couldn't see that there was any land underneath it, and it looked as if it was floating on the sea.

Turning back in her seat, she put her head down, and started to row towards the floating cathedral.

It would be somewhere to stop for a while, at least. She needed to sleep, and to find some food and water. Maybe she could find out where she was, so she would know which way to go on. Perhaps the ship that took her parents away had stopped here too. Someone might have seen them. But then, it looked to be only a little island. Zoe thought there probably wouldn't be anyone left on it.

She was wrong.

then

one

"What are you?" said one of them. "Cats?"

Zoe sat in the wet mud where the three had thrown her. She'd only been out of her boat for a little while before they'd jumped her. Her head rang from a fierce blow, and she felt confused. She was exhausted from rowing for so long.

"Nah, she's not Cats," said another. He was tiny, much shorter than Zoe. "Cats are afraid of water, right? Reckon she's Pigs. She looks good in the mud, anyhow!"

The third of them laughed.

"What are you? Pigs?" said the first one again. He was obviously in charge. He was good looking, short, though not as small as the little mouselike one.

Zoe looked at them dumbly. They weren't making any sense.

"Let's just scrag her anyway," said the third.

Their leader ignored this. He turned to Zoe again.

"Look, we're Eels, see? Eels. This is our place. So what are you?"

Zoe's head sang with pain, but dimly she understood what they were getting at.

"I'm . . . not from here. I'm from Norwich. Or what's left of it . . ."

They eyed her silently.

"She's lying," said the third. He looked stupid and mean. "Let's scrag her. She's Cats. I'm telling you. Or Pigs. Either way, let's just do her."

"Shut it, Spat," shouted the leader.

"Sorry, Dooby." Spat looked suddenly timid.

Dooby turned to Zoe.

"You're from over the water?" He said it slowly, suspiciously.

At last, Zoe fully understood something they were saying.

"Yes. I'm from Norwich But it's terrible there. There's hardly anyone left. They all went years ago. Some of us stayed and tried to make it work. But it's all over now."

Dooby seemed to ignore most of this. But he said, "You've got a boat then?"

"Yes, it's down . . . yes. I have." Something stopped Zoe from telling them where she'd hidden it. Not for the first time she wondered if leaving Norwich was the right thing to do. But then, she'd had no choice in the end.

"A boat!" said the mouselike one.

"Yeah. I heard, Munchkin," said Dooby. He turned back to Zoe. "Show us your boat, then."

Zoe hesitated.

"Or we'll scrag you properly," said Spat.

Zoe looked at Dooby. He seemed to be the boss.

"Spat's right," he said.

*

They stood looking at Zoe's tiny rowing boat.

She'd been lucky. She'd headed straight towards the island, and had found a good place to land. She wouldn't have been able to go any further, anyway. Then she'd dragged the boat up as far as she could, tucking it out of sight beneath a huge old tree that had its feet in the water. It was dying, but it had enough leaves left on it to hide her boat a little. It was as good as she could do. She'd decided to walk along the shore and find an easy way up to the cathedral.

And then coming around the corner of a ruined building her luck ran out. She walked slap into Dooby, Spat and Munchkin.

"You came from Norwich in that?" said Dooby, looking at the boat and shaking his head.

"Uh-huh," Zoe mumbled.

"What does it say on the side?"

"*Lyca*," said Zoe. "It's her name."

"Norwich is east, right? The big old city?"

"Yes, so?" asked Zoe, wanting some answers. She wanted to know where she was, and she was very hungry.

"You don't understand, do you? What's your name?"

"Zoe. Where am I? I just headed for that . . ."

"This is the Island of Eels. And we're the Eels, see? This is our island, and we're in charge. Now, Zoe, what we're wondering, is whether you're telling the truth. Whether you've really come across Udan-Adan. In that." He pointed at Zoe's little boat. "Norwich, you say? I didn't think there was anything left to the east. On the other hand you might be Cats, or Pigs. Or some other tribe. In which case you've come to try something on. Steal some food maybe, knock a few of us off, too, maybe? So which is it? Cats, Pigs? Horses? Or is this story of yours for real?"

Zoe wondered how she could convince them, and what would happen if she failed.

"Look, I've never heard of Pigs or Eels or anything. Norwich is lost now. I found this old boat and did it up. I just started to row. I ran out of food. Don't know when. Then I saw that thing sticking out of the water."

Zoe pointed over their heads, where behind them the huge old cathedral towered into the watery sky. Even though she stood on the land where it did, it still looked as if it was floating on the water that was all around them.

"I just kept rowing. It never seemed to get any closer. But I got here."

"So you're not Cats, then?" said Munchkin.

"We don't know that," said Spat.

"No," said Dooby, "but I believe her. So you don't belong to any of the tribes?"

"No," said Zoe.

"Well you do now," said Dooby. "As of now, you're an Eel. We could do with someone as smart as you."

"Smart?" said Spat.

"Yes, Spat. Smart. Smarter than you, anyway. Get all this way in that thing. She's got brains. Which are in short supply round here."

"So what?" said Spat. He stared straight at Zoe. "No one else has joined us before, have they? You always said it was dangerous. Why don't we just do like we did with everyone else who's come snooping. You said . . ."

"Don't tell me what I said, Spat."

Zoe saw Munchkin take a couple of steps away from the other two, automatically.

"Yeah, but Dooby, we always do 'em. Don't we? You said so . . ."

"I said, Shut It!" Dooby snapped at Spat. There was an uneasy silence for a while. Spat seemed to realize he'd pushed it a bit, and shrugged his shoulders. Zoe saw the anger slip off Dooby's face.

"Thank you, Spat. Anyway. You're not afraid of a girl, are you?"

Munchkin sniggered. Obviously pleased with himself, Dooby turned back to Zoe.

"So you're an Eel now, Zoe."

"But I don't . . ."

"I said, you're an Eel. No arguments. Unless you'd like to give the water a try without your boat."

Zoe shook her head, slowly. She was too tired and hungry to argue, anyway. She didn't even have the energy to wonder what sort of weird set-up she had walked into.

"Let's go back to base, then, lads."

They walked up the soggy hill to where the ruins of old stone walls appeared from the sea and led to the cathedral gates. Rising out of the water beside one of these old walls was a row of white posts.

They made their way in and around bits of fallen masonry, and then not long after, the main door to the cathedral was in front of them. It looked out across a large patch of muddy grass, in one corner of which stood an ancient cannon.

Two boys stood guarding the gateway. Past them was a long porch which led to the doors themselves. These had been reinforced with bands of metal and beams of wood. The two gatekeepers nodded at Dooby, meekly, though they were much bigger than him.

"All right, Dooby," said one. The other nodded. Neither smiled.

One of them shoved hard, and the door to the cathedral swung open.

"Well, Zoe," said Dooby, "welcome to hell."

Zoe had seen some unpleasant sights before, but nothing in Norwich was like this. Once more she began to wonder if she'd done the right thing in leaving at all. Huddled in small groups round smoking fires were the scraps of people. Their clothes were hardly more than rags, and were obviously the result of some fairly primitive sewing skills. Dooby and his two thugs were dressed like kings compared with the others in the cathedral. Zoe looked at her own clothes. She'd mended and patched them countless times, but they seemed almost new, now.

Once inside, Dooby turned to Spat and Munchkin.

"You've got things to do," he said, and they both went off into the gloom.

Zoe and Dooby walked up the aisle in the centre of the cathedral. Zoe couldn't help staring. She stared at the building that had once been magnificent. The floor was thick with dirt and heaps of rubbish. There were broken windows and broken furniture. It was a mess. Then Zoe stared at the people who were living in it. They were in just as bad a state as the building. So far she had only seen children, many of them younger than herself.

"Aren't there any grown-ups here?" Zoe asked. She felt it was the right thing to ask, though she didn't know why, it had been a long time since she'd had any adult help.

Dooby didn't answer.

Some of the people eyed Zoe suspiciously as Dooby walked her up the aisle, but most just ignored her. They looked underfed and wild. The smoke from all their fires drifted way up above in the vaults of the ceiling. Dooby was right. There was something infernal about the place. And it stank. The worst thing about it was the smell of rotten fish.

"Where do you grow your food?" Zoe asked, turning to Dooby.

Dooby laughed.

"Grow? We don't *grow* food."

"But what do you eat? On Norwich we had a few animals to breed from, and there were the allotments . . ."

"There's nowhere to grow food. And there's no food to feed animals, even if we had any. This island is only a mile long and half as wide. There's no space. It's all buildings and ruins of buildings. There's no room for animals, and anyway, you need two of things to breed, right? Two of every sort of thing. Well, we never have two of anything here. There's not enough to go round as it is, without looking after animals, too."

Then, as if he'd been saying things he shouldn't, Dooby added loudly: "But this is the best and biggest bit of land left in Udan-Adan, and we're going to keep it!"

He nodded at one or two people who might have heard him.

"What's Udan . . . ?" began Zoe.

"Udan-Adan. The *sea*. I thought you were supposed to be clever. If you're not then I don't . . ."

"Oh no," said Zoe quickly, "it's just we called it something different in Norwich. I meant, why do you call it that?"

Dooby stopped, as if puzzled. Then he pointed to a dim corner of the nave. Sitting on his own in the dark was a thin, wrinkled figure. He was talking to himself.

"See that man? He's called William. He's older than anyone else here. He says the sea is called Udan-Adan, see?"

William was the first adult Zoe had seen.

"Is he in charge?"

Dooby swore loudly.

"William?" he laughed. "William . . . in charge?"

Then he stopped laughing and grabbed Zoe's arm roughly.

"Listen to me, Zoe. I'm in charge here. Got it?"

He stared at Zoe, peering at her dark hair and eyes, her long oval face. He was obviously trying to scare her, and Zoe was scared.

But she said, "You're hurting my arm." She glared back at him, trying not to show her fear, but she felt her mouth quiver.

Dooby waited a moment longer, then let her go.

Zoe rubbed her arm.

"Aren't there any grown-ups here at all? Apart from William?"

"None that can tie their own shoelaces without worrying about it first," Dooby said chuckling. "Weak in the head, see? But even if there were some with a bit more brains, I'd still be in charge."

Zoe didn't doubt this. There was something about Dooby that made you do what he said. Something more than just his use of violence.

Zoe nodded at William, the old man in the corner.

"Does he know why this is happening?"

"Why what is happening?"

"Why the sea keeps on rising year after year. Where it comes from. If it will stop before there's nothing left."

"No one knows that," said Dooby. "William will tell you he does. But don't believe everything he says. He's mad."

Dooby laughed.

They walked on through the cathedral, until they reached the choir stalls. They were alone now.

"In Norwich, some of them said it wasn't the sea rising, but the land sinking."

"Doesn't make much difference, does it? All I know is that for longer than I can remember there's been the sea, coming to get us, and it's left us like this. Like rats on a sinking ship. But I'm not going to let it happen to me. Get some rest. Munchkin's getting some food for you. Find yourself somewhere to sleep later on. Because I want your help."

two

"Eels Island," Zoe said to herself. "I still haven't got a clue where I am."

There were so many questions she wanted answers to. She still had no idea how this ragged bunch of people survived. The island was little more than a tiny strip of mud in the middle of the sea.

All she knew was that she had finally left Norwich for ever. It had been her home for all of her short, strange life. The houses her parents had grown up in were both under water, now.

The house she'd been born in was a ruin. When it got too dangerous, they'd moved further into Norwich, to higher ground. Zoe was about seven at the time. It meant moving closer to other people. Zoe's parents didn't really like this. Other people generally meant trouble. As a result Zoe had had few friends. There had been one or two, but gradually their parents had given up and taken the supply ship to the mainland. Every parting had been hard for Zoe. After a while she made sure she never let herself like anyone too much. Because sooner or later, they'd leave too.

When they came to move house there were so few people left that there was plenty of space. And plenty of huge old houses to choose from.

"Which one do you like, Zoe?" her dad asked her.

They were standing at the end of a long street of large detached Victorian houses. All of them were unoccupied and they had all been looted too. What they needed was a roof over their heads, and a large garden to grow food.

Zoe looked carefully. Finally she saw a house that seemed a little more friendly than the others.

"That one," she said, and walked up to the gates.

"Seems okay to me," said her dad.

"Beats raising a mortgage, doesn't it?" said her mum.

After the night when her parents had sailed away without her, Zoe hadn't wanted to go back to the old house. It was too much. She'd spent a long time moving from place to place, but nowhere seemed right, so she always moved on.

One day at the allotments, Natasha suggested that they live together.

It wasn't long after Zoe had lost her parents, and the allotments were still being organized fairly well. There was a group of men and women who ran the allotments. They guarded it at night to stop people stealing the produce, and in the daytime they organized the work. For a few hours work you could earn yourself some vegetables, or some tinned food from their own store if there was nothing fresh to be harvested.

Zoe and her parents had made good use of the system while their own garden was not producing the goods. It worked fairly well for a few years. Not like later when things really started to go to pieces. Then there had been the fights, and people raided the allotments' food store rather than work.

Natasha's parents were dead, but she lived with some other people in an old block of flats. Zoe thought about her offer, but turned her down. She didn't like the set-up, and didn't like the other people. After that night on the shore, when she'd been separated from her mum and dad, something had changed in Zoe. The fight, the desperation, the fear on people's faces. She'd seen that everyone was only out for themselves and she knew no one really wanted her around anyway. They saw her as a rebel and treated her as a bit of an outcast. But that suited Zoe more or less. Let them think she was a tough loner, and they'd be more likely to leave her alone. There was some truth in it, but really, she was just too scared to trust anyone. She didn't want to *be* with anyone else. She just wanted her parents.

Then Zoe had found the boat. She'd been searching for food. Most places had been scavenged for all their tins of food already. Shops, warehouses and so on. So Zoe had been forced to try the most dangerous part of Norwich. Here there were some old warehouses that were in a really bad state. Bits of them were always collapsing, and there wasn't a bit of ground anywhere that wasn't covered with piles of rubble. It meant stumbling over heaps of fallen buildings, but at least Zoe was safe from one thing. Other people. She knew no one else came here, simply because of the dangerous buildings.

She hadn't found any food and was beginning to think of giving up for the day. Then she had spotted the side of a boat sticking up through the mud in the old warehouse. The warehouse was right by the sea's edge, which was just a few feet below it. Boat and mud must have been washed in together in one of the high points of the floods, and now the mud gripped the boat like glue.

Despite the danger from the ruined buildings all around her, she decided to make a new home for herself in the warehouse. She knew her mum and dad would have been horrified at the risk she was taking, but Zoe was more scared of other people than she was of falling bricks and stones. Later she would change her mind, as the building started to groan horribly in the slightest wind. Then, she would move her boat to the safety of the shed in the graveyard, but for now the old warehouse would be her home.

She moved house into a tiny room in the roof of the warehouse. It had been an office. Clearly no one had been there for a long time. The room must have been abandoned when the floods came, and there was still paperwork and office furniture sitting just as they had then. There were even some tins of tomato soup in a small cupboard in the corner. Zoe took this as a good omen, a sign that it was the right place to live. She was very hungry, and there and then she took the small pack from her back. It contained her most precious possessions: two water bottles, some bits of clothes, her compass, a bottle of vitamin pills she'd found, a pocket torch without batteries, a small blanket and an old book, in which she had meant to keep a diary, but hadn't. Finally, she found what she was looking for. She took her penknife and skewered the top of one of the tins of soup. Two holes; one to drink from and one to let the air in, so the soup came out more easily, just like her dad had showed her. She swigged the cold soup. It tasted great. She couldn't finish it in one go, so she carefully poured the rest into one of her water bottles, which was empty.

Water was the hardest thing to find – much harder than finding food. She used the bottles to collect whatever drinkable water she could find. Though occasionally she had found some bottles of mineral water, she mostly drank rainwater. She had hidden a series of tins and pans in various places. On rooftops and behind collapsing buildings – anywhere that no one else went. She would collect the water after every rainfall and store it in her bottles.

She felt safe in the office-room, and could keep an eye on the boat, too. She spent days digging it out, working as quietly as she could, just in case anyone was around. But she saw no one.

One night there was a terrible crash. Zoe's fragile room shuddered and the whole warehouse with it, as she realized that a nearby building was falling down. She clung to the floor and prayed that her room wasn't about to drop to the ground with it. The noise was awful, and seemed to take for ever to finish, but finally it did. She didn't sleep for the rest of that night, but lay awake listening to the sound of bricks occasionally slipping and then settling again.

Next morning she worked even harder on the boat. At the beginning, it was just something to do, to stop her from going crazy. But as she uncovered more and more of the boat she saw that it was in good condition, and she began to have real hopes of making it float again. Finally one day it was free, and she began to wash the slimy mud from it. As she washed the bow, a single word appeared: LYCA.

"Hello, Lyca," said Zoe. And she felt herself smile.

She'd set out to sea in Lyca, but now she was separated from her. A sudden fear took her, but fumbling in her pocket she found she still had the compass. It was all she had left.

Mentally she made a list of what to do. She would try and find out where she was. Then she'd get some food, and as soon as she could, she would go back to Lyca and escape. Try and find the mainland, and maybe then she would find some trace of her parents. One thing she knew for sure, she didn't intend to spend any time on Eels Island.

"There's something bad, here," she said quietly. "Lyca, I won't be long."

But she didn't get the chance to do anything.

Two girls came up to her almost as soon as Dooby left. They were both tall, and scrawny. They were dressed a little better than most, but their clothes were more a matter of improvisation than anything else.

"I'm Molly," said one of them. "This is Sarah."

"Hello," said Zoe.

"We've got to look after you," said Molly. She made it clear they hated the idea.

Molly turned to Sarah.

"Dooby says so, doesn't he?"

"I don't need looking after," said Zoe.

"Oh yes, you do," said Molly. "Dooby said we should stay with you all day, show you around. God knows why."

She turned to Sarah, again.

"Why Dooby didn't just have your boyfriend do her like all the others . . ."

"Yeah, my Spat's the man for the job," said Sarah, grinning.

"Stinking water rat, isn't she?" added Molly, looking at Zoe.

"And ugly, too," said Sarah, with spite.

Tempted as she was to hit her, Zoe put on a false smile.

"Well, maybe there's somewhere I can wash . . . ?"

"Go outside, take your lovely clothes off and wait for it to rain," laughed Sarah. Molly joined in.

"Silly little . . ."

Again, Zoe just smiled. If she couldn't get away for a

while, her only chance was to be accepted on the island. It seemed that the only person who didn't want her 'done' was Dooby, and that didn't make her feel any better. She wondered what he wanted her for.

"Well, if Dooby says you've got to show me around . . ." said Zoe.

"Yeah, all right," said Molly. "Come on, then. Get a move on."

The mention of Dooby's name brought an instant reaction, just the way Spat and Munchkin had jumped at what he said. This was different though. It wasn't fear, but something else. The two girls' voices softened when they spoke his name. By the time they'd shown Zoe half the way round the cathedral, she knew what it was. Love, pure and plain.

"This is where Dooby stands when he tells us what to do," said Sarah.

"Over there is Dooby's room," said Molly, pointing at a side chapel with a newly-made door.

"This gate here is where Dooby killed the last of the Dogs."

It was as though they were talking about a god, not a boy.

"Another tribe?" asked Zoe.

"Of course," said Molly, as if Zoe was stupid. "They tried a final raid on the island about a month ago. But Dooby made sure we were all right. His plans always work. This one Dog had sneaked inside, and Dooby saw him and stuck a pike into him."

"Then he chopped off his head and stuck it on a spike on the roof," said Sarah.

"Along with everyone else who's come visiting," added Molly.

Zoe couldn't tell if they were joking, or not. They were older than she was, but seemed like serious little children. Just in case they weren't joking, Zoe prayed that her parents' ship had come nowhere near.

If civilization was starting to leave Norwich, it had left here a long time before.

All day they kept Zoe busy. Once or twice she began to think they had relaxed a little towards her, but then she would ask something and they would laugh at her, or tell her about the fate of other 'visitors' to the island.

"So watch it," said Sarah, "or I'll get Spat to sort you out." She laughed.

Only once did they ask Zoe about herself.

"What are you doing here, anyway?" said Sarah.

In spite of herself, Zoe couldn't help answering. She was tired, and her defences were down.

"Looking for my parents."

"What do you mean?"

"I lost them . . . they left . . ."

"Without you?" Molly said, laughing.

"No, it wasn't . . ." Zoe began, but it was too late.

"They left her!" said Sarah to Molly.

"So why are you looking for them, then?" said Molly. "They obviously wanted to get rid of you!"

"No!" said Zoe, trying not to let them get to her.

"No? When was this, anyway?" asked Sarah.

"I don't know . . . a few months, maybe a year . . ."

Zoe wished she'd kept her mouth shut.

"A year! They left you a year ago and they haven't come looking for you!"

"See, they don't want her," Molly said to Sarah.

"Yes, they do!" Zoe shouted.

"That's right," Sarah said to Molly, "that's right. That's not the reason they haven't come to find her . . ."

Molly stared at Sarah, who seemed to be defending Zoe all of a sudden.

"The reason is . . ." Sarah continued, ". . . that they're dead!"

Sarah and Molly collapsed into laughter.

"No!" Zoe shouted. "No! It's not true!"

Tears started to burn her eyes, but the two girls just laughed more.

"Of course it is," they said, "Why else didn't they come to find you?"

They laughed again. Zoe tried to ignore them, but the awful possibility that they might be right was too painful.

Sarah and Molly stayed with Zoe for the rest of the day, until late evening. A horn blew, a strange low sound which echoed around the vast old building.

"Right," said Sarah, to Molly, "come on then."

They got up, and started to leave.

"Wait!" said Zoe. "Where are you going? What's that noise mean?"

"Curfew," said Sarah, without looking back. "Doors closed for the night."

And with that they were gone.

three

Zoe ate some foul food. She slept that night on a narrow wooden pew. She had no sheets, and had to use a mouldy hassock as a pillow, but she slept long and deep. She dreamed a strange mix of dreams. She was in a small boat, far out to sea. Her mother and father were there, too. And Dooby. And Natasha, who suddenly stood up and rocked the boat from side to side. Zoe screamed at her to stop, but the boat tipped and they all fell into the huge, freezing ocean.

She woke feeling a pain in her ribs, as though someone was kicking her. Someone *was* kicking her.

"Get up," said Spat. "I want to talk to you."

He gave Zoe another prod in the ribs with his boot.

"Stop it!" yelled Zoe, sliding off the pew. "What do you think . . ."

"Listen to me. I know you're a spy. I don't know where you're from. But you haven't fooled me, even if Dooby thinks you're . . ."

"Look, I told you, I don't know anything about Cats or Pigs."

"You know their names all right, don't you?"

"Only because you told them to me!"

Spat was looking like he meant trouble. He stepped up to Zoe's face.

"Don't be smart. You ain't so clever. If you think you can get in his good books then think again. I'm Dooby's eyes and ears round here, so don't get any big ideas."

"Hey, don't worry, I don't want to be anybody's nose-wiper."

Spat hit her hard in the stomach. Zoe hadn't been ready and went down easily. She crawled away, but Spat advanced.

"You little . . ."

Zoe had done her share of looking out for herself in Norwich, but she'd never really been much of a fighter.

Spat went to kick her again, but Zoe swung her legs and knocked Spat's standing foot from under him. He fell. This gave Zoe time to get up, but by the time she had, Spat was already coming at her again. Surprised, Zoe leapt backwards.

"Stop!" she shouted, but Spat was clearly in no mood to stop. He swung a fist and Zoe leant to one side. The blow caught her, but only just. It was enough to send her to the floor again, and then Spat was on her, legs pinning her arms to the hard floor, and his hands tightening around Zoe's throat. She tried to struggle, but she was just too weak from her sea-crossing. At the back of her mind was a desire to give up. It was such a struggle anyway these days . . .

Suddenly Spat flew backwards off Zoe's chest. Zoe tilted her head back to see Dooby looking at her upside down.

Dooby nodded at Zoe and then away, indicating that she should make herself scarce.

Zoe hobbled off, feeling the bruises already rising on her neck. As she went she heard Dooby approach Spat.

"I told you to keep your hands off her."

"Look, I'm sorry Dooby, but I . . . she's a spy . . . I'm sure of it."

He didn't have time to finish his sentence; Zoe looked back to see Spat being hurled across the floor again. Dooby wasn't large by any means, and really he was pretty thin. He clearly knew some hideous ways of fighting.

Zoe saw her chance. She hadn't got any food to take, but she wasn't going to hang around. It was time to find her way back to Lyca and get away. She crept down the length of the nave, trying not to be seen. Into her mind came her dream. She was convinced she was right about Natasha. Her subconscious was telling her so. Rocking the boat, and drowning them. And Dooby, laughing at it all, even as he went under. And her parents had just sat there, silently, and let it happen, while Zoe screamed at Natasha to sit down. They hadn't even tried to help her.

Zoe reached the great front gates of the cathedral. She wasn't sure if the gatekeepers would let her past, but she nodded at them and they made no move to stop her. They seemed not to care that she was there. She passed them and was in the open-ended porch that led away from the gates. It was dark, despite the wall of daylight facing her. Strange carvings were crumbling away on the pillars on either side of her. They disturbed her slightly, and she hurried on.

She was just about to step out of the porch when a voice spoke to her.

"Good morning, Zoe."

It was William, the old man Dooby had pointed out when she'd arrived. He was sitting in the darkness of the porch.

Zoe was unsure what to do.

"How do you know my name?" she asked suspiciously.

He laughed.

"They're all talking about you," he said.

"Who?"

He nodded back through the doorway.

"Everyone. No one can understand why you're not dead."

Zoe started to feel the fear coming at her again.

"Dooby seems . . ."

"Well, yes, Dooby," said William.

There was an uneasy silence for a while. Stupidly, Zoe felt embarrassed. She stood thinking of something to say so she could get away. The old man didn't seem as mad as Dooby had said. She'd have to be careful.

"So where are you going, then, Zoe?

"Nowhere," she said, hurriedly, "I was just going for a walk, and anyway, you know, it smells in . . ."

"No. I mean. Where are you going? Where did you come from? That sort of thing."

"Oh, well, you know, I'm happy to be an Eel. That's fine. If Dooby says so, you know, then . . ." she trailed off. "But I came from Norwich."

"Norwich stands trembling on the brink," said William, as if it made sense.

"Oh. Right," said Zoe.

"Or is that on the blink? I can never remember."

"Pardon?" said Zoe.

"If you do decide to leave . . ." said William. Zoe froze, trying to think of some lie to cover her intentions, but the old man went on.

". . . then don't try to fly, will you. There was this monk, see, who built a pair of wings. His name was Brother Elmer. This is a thousand years ago, now, I'm talking. He built some wings, like a bird. He thought he could fly. Well, he jumped off the tower, see?"

Stupidly Zoe asked, "What happened?"

"Well, he died, didn't he? Off you go, then."

"What?" asked Zoe.

Dooby was right. The old man was crazy, after all.

"I said, off you go. On your walk."

Zoe hesitated.

"Right. Thanks," she said. "Er . . . bye."

He didn't reply. She crept slowly out of the porch, as she went she heard him start talking to himself.

Zoe got to the corner of the porch, and then she ran till she had a stitch.

It was a cool, misty morning. She thought she knew where she was going, but in running had lost her way. Still, the island was small; it wouldn't take her long to find *Lyca*.

All around was the smell of wetness, but Zoe was used to that. Even though Norwich was much larger than this place, nowhere escaped the occasional especially high floods. At least they had enough high ground to grow some vegetables there, though. There was nothing here. Just the shells of old houses standing at or in the water's edge, but again, Zoe was well used to that.

Sometimes she wondered what life had been like before the sea came. Perhaps it hadn't seemed stupid to build so close to the sea, because perhaps the sea had been a lot further away. She didn't know, and she had never met anyone who'd been alive when the houses were built, though lots of people could remember when there had been much more land. Her parents had grown up in a different world, but a world that was already in trouble. Even then the sea level was rising. They never liked to talk about it much. Whenever she did manage to get something out of them about the old times, they went quiet for a while afterwards. Zoe had never known those times, though the really serious flooding only started when she was a little girl.

She checked around to see that no one was coming after her, then started to walk round the island. She noted the white posts rising from the sea. They had those in Norwich too; marking the sea-level, keeping an eye on its latest high tide. She shuddered; she'd been right to leave Norwich. There was limited time left that it could survive; same as this place. She'd just have to take her boat and get away. She knew there was land to the west. Lots of it. It was where most people had headed when the sea came. But that was long ago, and now there were no ships left on Norwich, nor anyone who would have known how to steer them. The stupid, stubborn few who'd stayed had slowly turned into people like those in the cathedral. Scrabbling around for wild food or doing a few hours at the allotments to earn something in return. If you were lucky, you might find an old store of food in tins. The labels were never legible, if they were there at all, but what was inside was usually still good. Except . . . Zoe remembered someone she knew who'd eaten from a tin that had gone bad. It was a risk you had to take.

She knew she probably didn't have much time, someone would come looking for her soon. But her luck was in. After only five minutes, she suddenly recognized where she was. It was the spot where Dooby, Munchkin and Spat had jumped her. She knew her way to her boat easily now.

She found the place. The boat had gone.

Instantly she realized why the gatekeepers hadn't stopped her. She also knew who had her boat. And she realized too why Molly and Sarah hadn't let her out of their sight the day before. She felt angry, stupid too. The sea was all around her; her boat was gone. There was nowhere to go. She was trapped.

 **four**

"Where's my boat?"

"Safe," said Dooby, calmly. "In a safe place."

"Where?" Zoe said again. "It's my boat, you had no right . . ."

"Yours is it? Pay for it, did you? Or maybe someone just gave it to you? No! You found it and took it, and now I've done the same."

"All right, I found it. But it didn't belong to anyone. It had been forgotten, and it took a lot of work to do it up. I spent weeks sneaking around the city finding the things I needed to mend it. I found the oars on the wall of a pub. No one else would have thought of that! So if it's anyone's it's mine!"

"Look, Zoe. I'm not taking it from you. Like I said, I want your help. And I want that boat, to get us, you and me, out of here."

"What?" asked Zoe. She was brought up short again. She wondered why she hadn't realized. It was obvious what he was after.

"I wouldn't tell that lot," he said, nodding through the door of the side chapel where they were sitting, "but this place is finished. I keep telling them we'll be all right, but time's nearly up for this place."

"You're right there," said Zoe. "How long have you been here?"

"Me? A few months now, I suppose. Why?"

Zoe shrugged.

"I just wondered . . ."

"How come I'm in charge? Because when I got here I found a bunch of animals, arguing and fighting. But they were all weak. I sorted them out. If they didn't like it, they went for a swim."

He paused. Zoe said nothing.

"You're the first good thing to come this way in a long time," Dooby said after a while, pushing his dark hair back into place.

Zoe didn't answer. For some stupid reason, she liked what Dooby had just said. It was the first time anyone had said anything nice to her in a very long time. But she told herself to be careful.

"You've got brains. Anyone with half a mind can see this place is living on borrowed time. This bunch of idiots have their uses, though. You wouldn't believe how many other people there are, other tribes who want this land."

"Pigs, Dogs?"

"That's right. Though the Dogs are no longer a problem . . . But there's others, too. Clinging to little blips in the sea like limpets. So they want my island. And at least this lot can fight. I'll say that for them."

"Didn't you try and make it work? On Norwich, it went well for a long time. We had food growing, rainwater collection. It was all organized for a bit. It really only started going to pieces a little while ago . . .''

"There's nothing here, Zoe. This place, it's no place to live. It's like being on a boat. A big boat, I suppose, but there's nowhere to go but the sea. No one can get off. And I don't let anyone on. Except you.''

Zoe's heart started to race. She knew how precarious her life was here.

"Well, if you're going to survive on a ship, you need to have the means of survival. Food. We were talking about this yesterday, weren't we?''

"Yes,'' said Zoe. She knew Dooby was horrid, had done terrible things, but she couldn't help feeling relief at having someone to talk to.

"If you want to eat chickens, you need two chickens to make more with, see? Two pigs to make more pigs, and so on. At least two of everything, and probably more like seven in case some of them die, or you have to eat them sooner, see?''

"And you haven't got anything here, have you?''

"Not any more,'' said Dooby. "We've got some stores of food, but there's not much left. I've been rationing things out as best as I can, but that lot don't understand. They think I can keep on giving them food for ever. We had some animals, but they're all gone now. We used to find seagulls' eggs, but even the birds have abandoned us now. I get some of them to fish from the shore, but . . . well, they don't catch much. Not enough anyway. So yes, I've been looking for a way out for some time.''

He paused, stroking his hair again.

"I have an engine. An engine for a boat such as yours.''

"An outboard motor? So why didn't you . . . you didn't have a boat, did you?''

"Exactly. And now you come along . . . well, it's fate, isn't it?"

Zoe didn't like the way this was going, but she played along.

"So where's my boat?"

"So, Zoe, I couldn't have everyone seeing it, could I? They might start to get ideas. So I had Spat and Munchkin move it to a safe little harbour. They're fixing the motor on to it, right now."

"But it's not big enough!"

"What for?"

"I mean, there wouldn't be enough room for you three, and me. Unless . . ."

"No, that's right. Like I said, the boat is just for the two of us, see? I don't need Spat and Munchkin, not now they've moved the boat for me. But I do need you, because you know how to work the thing. How to steer, how to find land again."

"And now I need you, because you won't tell me where it is."

"I knew you were smart," said Dooby grinning unpleasantly. "Oh and by the way, you won't say anything to anyone about this." He stopped smiling, and Zoe felt cold. He didn't need to say what would happen if she did.

She suddenly hated herself. She had caught herself liking the thought of escaping in a boat with him. She had caught herself liking him. But he had reminded her just in time of his real nature.

"Well," she said, risking a little edge in her voice, "what about everyone else? You're their leader, you can't just leave them . . ."

"Like you just left Norwich, you mean?"

"That was different."

"Was it?"

Zoe was silent.

five

Later that day, Zoe tried to find where *Lyca* had been moved to. After her conversation with Dooby, a new determination to escape had grown in her. She walked brazenly out of the gate this time. She felt that she didn't really care what happened to her now, she was just angry at the way Dooby was controlling her.

She searched as much of the shoreline as she could, but it was slow work. There were places where buildings stood at the water's edge, and she had to find a safe way through or round them. She knew from experience how dangerous these ruined buildings could be. Once the water had got under them they could become even more lethal to hang around.

The light was going, and as she got cold, her anger and determination began to slip away from her too.

Finally, she was barely able to see a few paces in front of her. Then she noticed a light flickering behind her. She turned to see Spat, with his usual mocking smile.

"Having fun?" he asked. "Curfew's in five minutes. Time for bed."

Defeated, Zoe went meekly back with Spat to the cathedral. They were just closing the doors when the horn sounded the curfew again.

That evening, food was served out to all the Eels. It was the most contact Zoe had seen between them. But even at this gathering they sat in huddles of two or three. Molly and Sarah and some older women stared at her as she sat down to eat.

"What's that smell?" said Molly.

"It's the stinky rat again," said Sarah.

"What've you been doing, stinky rat? Swimming in the slime?"

"Just look at her hair!"

They laughed.

Zoe's hair was no worse than theirs, but she tried to ignore them.

"Come and sit with me," said a voice.

She turned to see William, the old man, smiling at her. Gratefully, she sat beside him.

"Aren't you eating?" she said.

"I don't need any. More for someone else."

"But aren't you hungry?"

"All the time! Take no notice of them," he added, whispering so loud that everyone could hear. He nodded at the women who'd stared at her. They turned away.

"They don't trust you, that's all."

"I don't mean anyone any harm."

"But they don't know that. Where are you from? Why are you here? How can you do what none of us can?"

"What do you mean?"

"You came across Udan-Adan, didn't you? Even Dooby can't do that."

For the second time, Zoe changed her mind about William. He seemed totally normal to her now. He wasn't as old as she'd thought at first, either. Maybe fifty, maybe older. It was hard to tell. It had been dark in the porch when he spoke to her before. It was just that he was so much older than anyone else she'd seen in a long time.

"It's quite easy," said Zoe. "With a boat."

"A boat! Shall I tell you a story about a boat?"

"I'd rather ask you something else," said Zoe, but William wasn't listening.

"Well, there was a man called . . . called . . . oh I can't remember, but anyway, he built a boat, see?"

Zoe nodded.

"And then it began to rain, a lot. So, all the animals were getting wet, too, and he put them all aboard the boat, too. And it sank."

"That's a story?" asked Zoe. William was confusing, but even so his story reminded Zoe of something. A story her mother had once told her, perhaps. She tried to bring it out from the back of her mind, but she couldn't remember. William was still talking to her.

"That's just what happened. Here's another one. There was a doctor, and his name was . . . was . . . oh look, I can't remember! I'll tell you later. Anyway, he went somewhere, and there was a big puddle of water, and he stepped in it. So he never went there again. But that's nothing to what happened to . . ."

William went on, and Zoe smiled uneasily when he looked at her. Perhaps they were right after all; he was normal one minute, and mad the next. Some others had gathered around him now. They obviously enjoyed listening to his crazy stories.

". . . But when the dove came back with dry feet, they knew it was going to be all right. And that's how Utnapishtim, King of Shurrupak, became immortal."

They laughed at him as he finished his story.

When he paused, Zoe took her chance.

"William? Why is there so much water? Where is it coming from?"

He stopped short, and seemed to click back again. He spoke more slowly, which Zoe thought he seemed to do when he wasn't talking nonsense. There were about thirty people gathered around him now. He looked at them all carefully, and then spoke.

"You want to know? Then I shall tell you. It was too hot. It was too hot in the whole world, because people had too many fires. Always burning things. And the world got hotter and hotter and hotter."

Someone started giggling. William didn't seem to notice.

"This'll be a good one!"

"Shh!" said Zoe.

"Now the world, as everyone knows, is shaped like an egg. A big one."

More laughter.

"What's an egg, anyway?" someone joked.

"Shh!'

"And at each end of the egg, there were two huge lumps of ice. One at each end. Well, when it got hot, the ice started to melt. But that wasn't the real problem. You see, once the ice melted, the sea got warmer. Without all that ice, there was nothing to keep it cool, right? The world was getting warmer and so the sea got warmer too."

People were laughing, madly.

"And what happens when things get warmer?" William

asked, without looking at anyone in particular. He waited for an answer.

"I don't know, what does happen?" someone prompted.

"They get bigger."

There were huge hoots at this.

"The sea got warmer, and so it got bigger, which means it takes up more space, and that's why there's so much of it. That is why we are drowning."

He stopped. Zoe said nothing. Everyone else was still laughing hard.

"That's his best yet. Where does he get these loopy ideas from?"

"The sea *warm*? It's freezing!"

William smiled at Zoe. As he did so, she realized who she'd like to put in her boat when she made her escape.

No one was listening to William any more, except Zoe. His face was blank, his voice was grave and low.

"It's going to keep on coming. It hasn't finished yet. The whole world will go under before it's done, and wash the face of the earth clean."

He closed his eyes.

Zoe fought tears back.

"Unless," said William, thoughtfully. "You could build a really *big* boat . . ."

six

"Munchkin?"

Zoe thought she'd spotted him darting down the side of the nave. She'd been on the island for two days, and was starting to feel trapped. She thought about Dooby's threat. About not telling anyone his plan for them to escape. She had to admit it, he had scared her. But only Munchkin and Spat knew where her boat was. And she wasn't about to talk to Spat.

"Munchkin!" she said, louder, sure that it was him.

He stopped and cautiously came over to her. She nearly laughed whenever she looked at him; he was like a mouse. Small and nervous. But she had to remember he was as dangerous as the others. If Spat was Dooby's right hand, Munchkin was the left.

"What?" he said.

The directness of his question threw Zoe for a moment.

"Oh nothing, really," she said, trying to sound casual. She looked around. There was no one else anywhere near them.

"Well, I've got stuff to do for Dooby." He started to leave.

"Wait!" she said. "I was thinking."

"What?"

There was nothing else she could think of to say. She had to ask him, or he would go.

"You moved my boat, didn't you? I thought maybe you could show me where . . ."

Munchkin looked as if she'd said something awful, and began to back off again. But faster this time.

"I'm not supposed to talk to you about your boat . . ."

"No wait, please," said Zoe, "I just want to know if it's all right. That's all."

Munchkin hesitated. He thought for a long time, trying to make up his mind about something. Zoe began to regret mentioning it.

"How should I know?" he said finally.

"Well. Is it still floating?" asked Zoe, genuinely anxious.

"Oh, yes. But that's enough. I've got things to do for Dooby, and he doesn't like it if I get things wrong."

Zoe could imagine what that meant.

"Don't any of you stand up to Dooby?" she asked.

The shocked look came onto Munchkin's face again.

"Oh no! He's the boss. Anyway, without him, we'd all be in big trouble. No one else would know how to organize things, anyway, he looks after us, see?"

"He looks after you?" said Zoe.

"Yes. You don't know what it was like before he came . . ."

"What do you mean?"

"It was terrible, we were nearly starving. And the arguing . . ."

"So how did he get here? On a boat?"

"Yes, on a boat, with some others."

"Who?" asked Zoe.

"Molly. Spat. You know. Just some of the others."

"And Dooby was in charge of this boat?"

"Oh no. Even he doesn't know how boats work. He was just one of the people on it. There was a man. He was in charge."

"So what happened?"

"What do you mean?" asked Munchkin, suspiciously.

"Well, why did Dooby stay?"

"The boat was damaged. It was sinking. They tried to land on the island, and there was a fight. The man who drove the boat was killed. And then it sank, anyway. So they were stranded here. Dooby took control, then. Before he came, it was awful; everyone fighting everyone else. Dooby made it better. First thing he did was to get everyone to get what they could from the ship. It was stuck in the mud for a week, but sinking slowly. Then a storm dragged it off one night. There were loads of stores. Food, blankets. Before the storm we got most of it ashore and stored it in the cathedral. Dooby did it. He saved us."

A thought occurred to Zoe.

"How long ago was this? There wasn't a man and a woman on the boat, was there? A couple . . . the woman looks just like me, but older, and . . ."

She stopped. She saw how pointless her questions were.

"It was a long time ago. Dooby's been in charge since then, without him, it'd be like it was before. It would be awful."

She saw that he meant it. She thought about telling him that Dooby was intending to betray him, and Spat. Then she thought better of it; she couldn't take the risk.

"But he's a bully!" she said, instead. No matter how nasty

Munchkin was, she didn't like the way Dooby was manipulating everyone.

"I've got to go now," said Munchkin, and he went.

He darted round a corner, and Zoe followed, but Munchkin had completely vanished. There was a corridor leading away from her, with a door at the end, but he couldn't have got there in that short a time. There was nowhere else he could have gone. Zoe shook her head, puzzled, but she was really worrying about something else.

If Munchkin told Dooby what she'd asked she'd be in big trouble.

She could only hope that he'd keep it to himself.

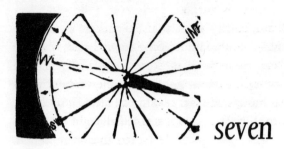 seven

Zoe felt at a dead end. She wanted to escape, but she didn't want to escape with Dooby. She knew that the second she stopped fitting into his plans her life would be at risk. She didn't know where *Lyca* was. She didn't even know where *she* was. Her only hope was to work on Munchkin. If she could just find out where her boat was being kept, then she had a chance.

In the meantime, she decided to at least try and find out where the island was. Then her compass could be of some use when she came to get away. There was only one person Zoe felt like talking to: William. And Dooby had said William knew everything there was to know, so she went looking for him. He had also said William was mad, but Zoe had few choices.

As she went, she saw Munchkin creep out from Dooby's room. She hoped he hadn't said anything to Dooby. That she'd asked about her boat. She'd been stupid to say anything, at all. Munchkin could have told him everything by now.

The island was small anyway, she'd find her boat soon enough by herself, given the chance to look for it. And when she did, she wasn't going to hang around.

She found William, sitting alone as usual, in one of the side chapels. The multi-coloured light from a stained glass window fell across his face. He looked like something from a stained glass window himself. Fortunately for Zoe, he was in one of his more normal moods. He was reading a battered old book. Its cover was torn, but the rest of it seemed all right.

"Hello again, Zoe," he said. He patted the stone bench. She sat down next to him, but he kept on reading. Zoe tried to think of something to say to get him talking.

"What are you reading?" she said.

"This is my favourite book," William said.

Zoe was getting nowhere.

"Why?" she asked.

"Oh, well, the man who wrote these poems has the same name as me, see? Funny isn't it?"

He went on reading for a moment, then suddenly shut the book. Zoe jumped.

"So. What can I do for you?" William asked.

Zoe sighed with relief.

"How do you know I want something?"

"People generally do, when they come to talk to you. No time for small talk, is there?"

"No," said Zoe, "I suppose not."

"Well?"

"Well, it's just that, I don't know where I am and I don't know where my parents are or if they're even . . . and I don't know what to do about Dooby, and I don't know where my boat is . . ."

"Right," said William, "I see."

"I mean, I'm just fed up. Why does everything have to be so difficult? So scary?"

"Hmm," said William.

"I mean, why is this even happening?"

"What?"

"The sea rising."

"Well, I thought I told you about that the other night."

Zoe paused. Not wanting to offend him, she said, "Oh, I know, but I mean, when did it start? Will things always be like this?"

"Ah," said William. "Well, Zoe. It started a long time ago. I was about your age, I suppose, when it began. Back then, you could walk from here in any direction for fifty miles and not meet the sea."

"Have you lived here all your life then?"

"Of course," said William, as if it was obvious, but Zoe knew that a lot of people must have come and gone; been made to come and go on the island, in that time.

"Do you mean there was no sea between here and Norwich?"

"Norwich? That's where you're from, isn't it? That's right. You could drive there, in a car, I mean, in an hour or so."

Zoe's parents had told her about cars. Their remains littered every street in Norwich.

"Didn't anyone tell you this before?" asked William.

"Yes and no," said Zoe, "My parents told me about a lot of things, but mostly stuff I needed to know about."

"How old would your parents be?"

"I don't know, really. About forty, I suppose. Why?"

"They'd just about remember things properly then. Before the sea came, I mean. Even then it was a while before it got really bad. But it just kept on coming. I don't think anyone took it seriously enough. By the time they did, it was too late. The world couldn't cope any more, by then. Your parents probably told you this, though."

"They told me there didn't used to be the sea all around, but that was it really. We were too busy just getting on with things apart from that. Surviving. I know there's the main part of the country still out there, to the west."

"West, yes. There's a feeling I get when I look to the west."

"What do you mean?"

"Oh nothing, I don't know. Just some words from the past. West is where the sun sets, isn't it?"

"So then what happened?" asked Zoe, anxious that William was about to change the subject.

"Well, it was just small floods. The panic they caused! The weather went up the spout, and lots of rivers burst their banks. But it was nothing to what happened when the sea started to come. Bits of the coast, they went first. They fell into the sea. And the sea rose some more, and the lowlands went under. That's when it really got bad. When things started to . . . We heard reports from all around the world on the news. Everywhere the sea was covering the land. Then we didn't get any more news."

Zoe didn't understand a lot of what he was saying, but she didn't interrupt.

"Then things got worse round here too. Holland went, then we got cut off. You wouldn't believe the floods. The water would only be rising slowly, I suppose, but it would hold itself back and then come with a charge when the land couldn't take it any more. The people! People from all over coming and going. We just weren't ready and the country couldn't take it. The world couldn't take it, I suppose, but by then we had no idea what was going on elsewhere. We were on our own . . ."

He stopped, and was silent for a long time. It clearly hurt to remember.

Zoe tried to imagine what the world was like when William was a boy, before the sea started coming. It was a world of which she only knew the shadows. The boxes of things she didn't understand, with happy faces smiling on the side of them. The ruins of cars rusting in the streets, all useless now. The derelict buildings made unsafe by the water swelling up into the ground beneath them like into a sponge . . .

"Were you happy, then?" asked Zoe.

"Well," said William, slowly, "about as happy as I am now."

He looked Zoe straight in the eyes, and smiled.

She looked away.

"William, where is this place? I need to know so I know where to head when I go."

"I would say you're about halfway between Norwich and the mainland. The sea's slowed down recently, have you noticed that?"

Zoe shook her head.

"Well, anyway. This island became a real crossroads. People heading west, people heading north. It was a mess. Then that young Dooby came along."

"You don't like him too, do you?" asked Zoe, surprised.

"He's nothing to do with me. I was here before he came, and I'll be here when he goes."

Zoe started to speak, but William saw what she was thinking.

"Oh, he'll go, all right. Leave this lot to it."

"How do you know?"

William didn't answer.

Instead, he said, "So what about your parents, then? You're on your own?"

Zoe told him the story of that horrible night.

"They left you? That's terrible."

"No!" said Zoe angrily. "They didn't leave me. It was an accident. There was no choice."

"I see," said William. "Well, I suppose it wouldn't be the only time it's happened. Same stories over and over again. Over and over."

"You never saw them here did you? Maybe a year ago? Something like that?"

William shook his head.

"How would I know?" he said, though not unkindly. "No one uses proper names any more, do they? What's your last name, anyway?"

For a second, Zoe was stunned. She thought she had forgotten it. Her own name. With a struggle, she fished in her memory.

"Black," she said, eventually.

"Really? Black? That's nearly the same as mine . . . Blake, see?"

He showed Zoe the name on his book again.

But Zoe wasn't listening. How could she nearly forget her own name?

"Well, anyway," William went on, "if you head west, you'll find dry land again sooner or later."

"Is that the best you can do?" snapped Zoe. "I can't just row off into the middle of nowhere again. I can't!"

William turned and looked at Zoe, then away. He got up.

"William," she said quickly, "I'm sorry. Look, I've got a boat. You know that, don't you? It's how I got here, and it's how I'm going to get away."

"Yes. You get away," said William. "In a boat. Good idea."

"Come with me!" said Zoe. "I'll go west, where there's higher ground."

"West. That's right. Your salvation lies to the west of Udan-Adan . . ."

"I'm going to go and look for Lyca tonight, when everyone's sleeping."

"Lyca, you say?"

"It's just the name of my boat, that's all . . ."

Zoe could see the change in William happen before her eyes. He was starting to lose it again, slipping off into his other world.

"You think it's just the name of your boat? Lyca, Zoe, is the little girl lost.

> Do father, mother weep,
> where can Lyca sleep?
> Lost in desert wild,
> is your little child . . ."

"William! You're not listening . . . Come with me. I'll get you out of here!"

He looked at her sharply.

"Why would you want to do that?"

Zoe was puzzled by his question, but it was a good one. She had made it a rule not to trust anyone, and it had seen her through all right. William obviously felt the same way.

"Why?" William said again. "Why me? There's plenty of

people you could take. Younger, stronger, more use to you than I would be. Why put your trust in me?''

"I don't know," said Zoe. "I just want to."

Suddenly, shouts and the sounds of scuffling came from the porch of the cathedral. Zoe rushed to the door of the chapel where she and William had been sitting. At the door she froze. She could see well enough from there what was happening.

"A spy!"

"It's a Cat!"

"Dooby! Fetch Dooby! We've found a spy."

A young man was being pulled into the building by four Eels. He looked terrified. Zoe wouldn't have known he wasn't another Eel, if he wasn't being dragged along by his arms. Dooby, hearing the fuss, came out of his room to meet them. It was no surprise to Zoe to see Spat was among the four who'd found the spy.

Spat took hold of the spy's collar and threw him on to the cold stone floor.

"Dooby!" he said. "We found this Cat. Sneaking around outside!"

"Did he have a boat?" asked Dooby quickly. A little too quickly, Zoe thought.

"I've sent Tolly and Soup to search the whole shore; but there's no sign of one. They must have dropped him and then scarpered."

Dooby turned on the spy, who lay quivering on the flagstones.

"Is that true?" he snapped.

Bravely, or stupidly, the Cat said nothing. Dooby swung his boot into him. Zoe looked away.

"Take him into my room. Let's find out what he's up to."

They took him away. Spat and Dooby followed.

It was late. Zoe went to the pew she was using as a bunk, but she couldn't sleep. Screams and chokes from Dooby's room floated out into the cathedral. Horrified, Zoe decided to try to have another look for her boat. But at the gate she was stopped.

"You know the rules," said the gatekeeper, "No one allowed out after curfew."

She hadn't heard the horn somehow. She must have been too deep in her conversation with William.

Zoe crept miserably back to her bunk, and tried not to listen to the noises of the Cat. He had looked so pitiful. She stared at the ceiling high above her, feeling guilty for doing nothing, and terrified at what would happen to her if Dooby didn't have plans for her and her boat. Her mind began to drift to her parents, and to her old life on Norwich. At least it was something she could focus on, to try and block out the sickening noises. Suddenly, as she gazed up at the ceiling, she saw something move. The ceiling was made of painted panels. Lots of people in various scenes. Zoe guessed they told bits of a story, but she didn't know what it was. But she was sure that part of one of the pictures had just moved. Then she saw it again. It was a light, somewhere above the ceiling. A light moving round and shining through a tiny hole in one of the panels.

Her mind made a connection to something that had happened earlier that day. Somehow she knew what, or rather who it was.

eight

Zoe got up from her bunk. Checking to see that no one was watching her, she went back to the corridor where she'd spoken to Munchkin that morning. It was darker than ever now, and she stumbled around for a long time. At last her eyes got used to the darkness and she could pick out the shape of the walls beside her. But still, she couldn't find what she was looking for.

She tried feeling her way all along the walls, but found nothing. She gave up. Sliding down the wall, she sat on the floor, and decided to stay there for a while; the noises from Dooby's room were almost inaudible here. That was something, at least.

She began to doze. Then, as if it was a dream, a line of light appeared in the darkness opposite her. She wondered if she had gone crazy, as the beam of light grew in front of her eyes. It was only a few paces to the left of where she sat. It hung motionless in the air for a moment like a sword of fire. Then it grew out sideways at the top and bottom, and got fatter. Finally she realized what she was looking at.

It was a small door opening in the wall, with a light behind.

She was right. A moment later she saw Munchkin step down from the door halfway up the wall. Zoe was terrified he'd see her, but Munchkin's eyes had been exposed to the flickering light of his candle, and Zoe was still sitting in a dark corner. She watched as Munchkin carefully closed the door behind him. Zoe saw why she hadn't found it. Even staring straight at it, it was hard to see where the door was, now that it was shut.

As soon as Munchkin was convinced he'd shut it properly, he blew his candle out. Zoe was sure this was something only he knew about, something he wanted to keep that way. He was moving extremely quietly and slowly, and from the care he had taken to make sure the door was invisible again, she knew this was one thing no one else knew about, not even Dooby. Even as she sat there in the darkness, an idea came to her, and her heart started thumping so hard, Zoe thought Munchkin would hear it.

He was so close that Zoe could smell the reek of smoke from the extinguished candle. She held her breath, thinking he was still there, but when she heard his feet shuffle at the end of the corridor, she realized that he had quietly walked away.

Zoe thought for a moment. She felt that there might be a chance of a bargain to be had. If she could find out why Munchkin's hideout was such a secret, she might be able to bargain with him, get him to tell her where Lyca was being kept. In return, she wouldn't tell Dooby about Munchkin's hidey-hole.

But she couldn't do anything about it now; she didn't have a light. She'd have to come back when it was light; some time when Munchkin was doing something else.

She put her hand out against the wall, and counted her footsteps to the end of the corridor. She had to know how to find the place again.

The following morning, Dooby called everyone into the centre of the cathedral to make an announcement. He climbed into the pulpit.

"We can expect an attack," he said. "The spy was very helpful. He tells us that the Cats are planning an attack in a few days time. We must be ready for it when it comes. I will be discussing preparations for our defences with Spat and Munchkin. When I have decided what we need to do they will inform you of your jobs. That's all for now."

Dooby, Munchkin and Spat went off into Dooby's room. Zoe looked around. She saw Sarah and Molly standing nearby. Sarah was talking loudly about Spat, making sure no one would forget he was her boyfriend. As if that were possible. Everyone seemed quite calm about the news, but Zoe's heart was racing. And then it stopped. Zoe had seen something that filled her with fear. She was watching Sarah showing off to the others. Then she saw her pull something on a cord around her neck from inside her dress.

Attached to the cord was a pendant, a very unusual one. The cord it was strung on was normal enough, but the piece of jewellery itself was unmistakable. It was a big silver disc engraved with a pattern of the points of the compass, not just the four main points, or the four more between them. This compass had sixteen big arrows and then another sixteen minor points marked by fine lines. Zoe knew it in detail without needing to see it more closely. Because it had been her mother's.

Sarah stood pretending to clean it, but really it was just part of her showing off. Something broke inside Zoe, and she charged at Sarah.

Zoe practically threw herself at her.

"Where did you get that?" she yelled.

Sarah had been taken by surprise, and for a moment was too stunned to say anything.

"It doesn't belong to you!" Zoe shouted. "Give it to me!"

"Get off me!" Sarah yelled back, pushing Zoe away.

Zoe fought to grab the necklace from Sarah's neck, but she was held back by some of Sarah's friends.

"Get lost, you little creep!" yelled Sarah. "Get your hands off me!"

Zoe wrestled with them.

"Let go of me!" she screamed. "Give me that! It's not yours!"

"Stop her!"

"Someone shut her up!"

"Where did you get it?" Zoe shouted. "Tell me!"

Zoe nearly broke free, but Molly came over and hit her across the face twice.

"Shut up! You're crazy . . ." She hit Zoe again, and Zoe had had enough. She sank into the arms holding her. They let her drop to the floor, where she lay crying.

Sarah came up to her.

"Why do you want to know, anyway? What's got into your crazy little head?"

Zoe shook her head. If she told Sarah it was her mother's they'd never leave her alone. Besides, the fact that Sarah was wearing it was all Zoe needed to know.

As if Sarah knew what she was thinking, she said, "Spat got this for me. It was his present to me, see? And the previous owner no longer has any need for it."

She laughed. The others joined in.

"Come on," she said to them, "let's go. Stinking little rat . . ."

They left Zoe huddled on the floor, muttering insults at her as they went.

Zoe felt a hand on her shoulder. She looked up. It was William.

"Zoe, my dear." His voice was kind and calm.

Zoe just shook her head, dumbly.

"What was that all about?" William asked.

Still Zoe only shook her head.

"Don't go looking for trouble, Zoe. Even Dooby won't look after you for ever . . ."

"You don't understand . . ." Zoe said through her tears. "That pendant. It was my mum's . . . it is my mum's. I'm sure of it."

"Oh Zoe . . ." began William.

"No!" said Zoe firmly, "I know it is!"

"But Zoe, I was going to say . . . That's good."

"Good? How can it be good? If Sarah's got it, and Spat gave it to her, then . . ."

"No. That's just the point. Spat didn't give it to her. He wasn't even here when she got it. She just says he did because she thinks he loves her. I know where she got it. Everyone does. She's so stupid that one. So vain . . ."

Zoe couldn't understand what William meant.

"You're not making sense. Tell me!"

"A ship came by. Last one we saw. Sarah got it from a woman on board."

"What? When was this?"

"Last year some time. I don't . . . it's so hard to keep track, you see. Swimming on the open sea . . ."

Zoe wanted to keep William on the subject.

"Did you see the woman who gave it to her?"

"Oh," he said, "oh. She didn't *give* it to her."

"Then . . . ?"

"She swapped it for some food. That's why Sarah's so stupid . . . what use is jewellery here? She gave food for it. Food, the only thing that's any use."

William started laughing, and despite herself, Zoe did too.

"That could have been my mum, that's just like her . . . but did you see her?"

"No. No, it was her husband who did the deal. There was a little boat, see?"

"But they didn't take anyone with them? Why didn't you go?"

"I think they'd sized us up pretty quickly. They said they were full, that they'd come back for us. Of course, they never did . . ."

That sounded right to Zoe. The captain hadn't even turned back for her. When he saw the bunch of savages on Eels Island he must have wanted to keep well away.

"But why did they stop at all?" asked Zoe.

"What?"

"Why did they stop here at all? Why didn't they just keep clear and head on for the mainland?"

William shrugged.

"They said they needed food. There was none on board and some of them were near to death from it. They didn't even land. A few of them just rowed close by in a boat. Some of us went down to the shore."

"Wait. Was this before or after Dooby came?"

"Oh before. He'd never have let anyone swap food for jewellery . . ."

"But why did she?"

"Vain, see? They shouted across to us. Food! We'll pay you for it! Everyone told them to get lost! Take us with you and we'll bring some food, they said. Then the men in the boat said they were full, that they'd come back, like I told you. They never did, of course . . ."

"So what about Sarah?"

"Ah. Well, Sarah was different. She waded out to the boat with this great armful of food, and then she came back with that necklace thing . . ."

"But didn't anyone try and stop her?"

"No," said William, "like I said, this was before Dooby got here. There was no one with any brains at the beach, see? Those that were, you know . . . ? A bit simple. They just watched her do it. There was a real fight about it later, though. People tried to get it off her, but she kicked and screamed till they left her alone. But she said she made the men in the boat promise to come back for them all, when they weren't full. Never did, but then you know that, eh?"

Zoe's mind was reeling. This was the first news she heard of her parents in a very long time, but it was good news. They'd been all right when they'd passed the island. They hadn't stopped, but gone on to the mainland.

"They must be all right," Zoe said to herself, but then doubt came into her mind again. If they were okay, why hadn't they come back to look for her? Perhaps it wasn't her dad who'd been in the boat and swapped Mum's jewellery for food. Maybe it was someone else, maybe the only reason they had it to swap was because . . .

"No!" said Zoe aloud. "They're okay. I know it."

She told herself that seeing the pendant was a good thing,

she wouldn't believe otherwise. But she had to find her parents, and to do that she had to get off this stinking little island.

nine

Zoe knew time was running out. She would have to find Lyca fast, or she was going to get caught up in a fight she wanted nothing to do with. Her fate would become a matter of chances then.

With Munchkin occupied for a couple of hours at least with Dooby's meeting, Zoe decided to find his hideout. She was convinced she could do a deal with him, just like her parents had with Sarah. They traded food for a useless bit of jewellery. She would trade information for silence. Her boat for not telling Dooby about Munchkin's lair. But to do that she had to find it first.

She had to do it without being seen by anyone, and that was one of the things about the inhabitants of the cathedral, they were always watching. It was even hard to see everyone who might be watching her, many of them clung to the dark corners, hidden from sight.

Still, the urge in her to explore was too strong to ignore. As far as she could tell, no one was taking any notice of her. As calmly as she could, she took a burning candle from the side wall of the cathedral and headed for the corridor she'd sat in the night before. In daylight it was surprisingly easy to find the hidden door. She counted the number of steps she'd taken before, and there it was in front of her. Still, if you didn't know where to look, you'd probably never find it.

She gave it a push with her hand, and it sprang back slightly. She put her fingers round the crack and pulled. The stone swung towards her. A narrow spiral staircase struck out upwards into the huge old stonework of the walls. Shoving the smoky candle in front of her, she climbed into the hole.

There was an iron handle fixed into the back of the stone door. It was smooth and cold. She pulled the door to behind her. Her candle flickered gold on the stone and she began to climb into the roof of the cathedral.

On her way up there were a couple of turnings that she could have taken. A junction here and there with other passages led away into the cramped darkness. But it was obvious which way Munchkin went; even in the gloom of her candle-light Zoe could see where the side passages were thick with dust. As she climbed up the steep stone stairs she could see they had been swept by the regular passage of feet. Munchkin's feet.

Just as she began to wonder when the climbing would stop, the stairs ended abruptly. There was a low tunnel that ran away from her. Its floor curved slightly upwards, and she guessed she was right up in the roof now, in some space at the edge of the vaulting. She walked down the tunnel, choking from the smoke of the candle in the confined space. At the end was a wooden door about three feet high. She pushed it open and found herself looking into Munchkin's lair.

Almost immediately she saw the hole in the floor that

she'd spotted from below. She realized she'd have to be as quiet as Munchkin or someone might hear her. She stepped down the slight step into his secret world. At first Zoe thought there was nothing there. There was a mattress, but no other furniture. She held her candle in front of her. There was something on the far wall. With a jolt, Zoe saw it was a map. Eagerly she went to get a closer look, but something moved to her left. She spun and gave a little cry.

There, on a battered wooden box, was a rusty cage. In the cage was a rat, standing on its back legs and sniffing the air. It tilted its head to one side, as if waiting to be fed.

"What are you doing here?" said Munchkin from behind her. His voice was quiet, but Zoe could tell he was angry. She remembered that if he were to shout, he'd be heard from below.

He stepped forward.

"I didn't mean any harm," Zoe whispered.

"You're lying!" said Munchkin, a little too loudly. He shrank at the sound of his own voice.

"No!" said Zoe, but she knew that he was right.

"What are you doing here?" he said again. He moved in and shut the door behind him. Zoe took a step back, still holding her candle firmly. She tried to work out whether he'd risk attacking her up here. Munchkin seemed to be trying to work out what to do, too. For a long time they stood watching each other carefully, like animals about to fight. In the cage the rat dropped to its paws and ran up and down the length of its home. It suddenly gave a loud squeak.

"Shh, Rat!" said Munchkin.

"You must have to be really careful with noise. Up here, I mean," Zoe tried.

"You shouldn't be here," said Munchkin, but Zoe thought he sounded less cross.

"Does he think you've brought some food?" asked Zoe, nodding at the rat.

"What?"

"Your rat. Have you come to feed him?"

"There's never enough food," said Munchkin. "But I give Rat what I can spare, see?"

"He's really . . . nice," said Zoe. Lying again, she thought. She wasn't actually afraid of rats. There were plenty of them around, after all. It was just that this one was in a pretty bad state. It had patchy fur, and it looked as if it had chewed off its own whiskers. It had the sort of mangy looking tail that only sick rats get.

"I know he's not much to look at," said Munchkin defensively.

"You should let him out sometimes. Do you let him out?" asked Zoe, realizing as she said it that it might not be a tactful question to ask. But it was all right.

"Oh yes," he said, "but sometimes it's such a job to get him back in the cage. He got out of the door the other night and then I was hours chasing him all through."

"Are there lots of these passages, then?" asked Zoe.

"Oh yes," said Munchkin, but then he remembered something. "You shouldn't be up here."

Zoe cursed herself for bringing the conversation back to that.

"Why not?" she said.

Munchkin looked at her.

"This is my place," he said, "and you shouldn't have come up here."

"Look, Munchkin. I'm sorry. I didn't mean any harm. I just want to know where my boat is . . ."

"Well, it's not up here, is it?" He didn't mean to be funny.

Munchkin turned to look at his rat. He started whispering to it quietly, as if he had forgotten Zoe was there.

"All right, Rat? Been a good boy, have you?"

"Look, Munchkin. Please, tell me where my boat is."

"No," he said, without turning round.

"Please tell me. And if you do tell me, then I won't tell Dooby about this place . . ."

Then he did turn round.

"Please don't do that," he said quietly.

"Well, just tell me where my boat is, and . . ."

"I can't," Munchkin said even more quietly. "Please. Don't tell him."

He looked at Zoe, and she saw the fear on his face. She looked away.

She knew she'd never be able to get him into trouble. And she hated herself for even trying to threaten Munchkin. She would be just as bad as everyone else if she started that kind of thing.

"Munchkin," she said, shaking her head, "what are you doing working for Dooby?"

"Mind your own business," he said, but it was without anger.

"Your meeting was over quickly."

"Dooby's got it all under control," he said. Then he added, "Please go."

"Okay," she said. "Listen, I promise I won't tell anyone about this place. Or Rat. Okay?"

He nodded.

As she stepped backwards through the small door, she had to ask one more question.

"Munchkin, where's that a map of?"

He looked at it for a second.

"That's here, that is. Years ago. See? There's no water anywhere. Just a couple of rivers. This brown bit here, that's the island now. And that cross is the cathedral."

"Wow," said Zoe. Her spirit leapt. She could see land, lots of land. Land all the way from the island to Norwich to the sea, miles and miles away. And in the other direction, the map finished before any sea appeared.

"Where did you get it?" she asked.

"It was my mum's."

His words reminded Zoe of her mother's pendant. She wanted to get it back badly, but knew it wasn't worth the fight. She already knew she would have to let it go, no matter how much it hurt.

"Have you got parents?" asked Zoe, stupidly.

"Not any more," said Munchkin. "Have you?"

"Yes," said Zoe. "No. I don't know, really."

There was an end to their talk.

"Please go, now."

Munchkin seemed to have gone back into his shell.

"Munchkin, I couldn't come and have a proper look at the map, some time . . ."

"Please go."

Zoe knew she was taking a risk. If she pushed Munchkin too much, and he got angry, someone might hear them. But she had to get a better look at the map.

"Just quickly, to make a copy or . . ."

"Go!" said Munchkin.

She nodded her head.

"Okay, Munchkin," she said, giving up. She couldn't take the risk of someone hearing them. She decided to come back another time.

She ducked backwards through the little door.

"Your boat," said Munchkin, suddenly. "There's a shed. On the west side. But it's locked. Only Dooby has a key."

"Thanks, Munchkin!"

She rushed back into the room and nearly kissed him. But Munchkin looked so shocked that she backed away again, smiling.

"Thanks," she said.

She left Munchkin in peace. Hope had started to surface in Zoe's heart. She knew her parents had got as far as the island, and had got away, too. Her boat was all right. She knew where it was. She had her compass. She just had to break the lock on the shed and she could get away.

"If I can just get a proper look at that map," she said to herself. But there was hope. She might be able to talk Munchkin round, to let her have a decent look at his map. Talking to Munchkin, she'd felt him warm slightly. It had been almost a normal chat, like one friend to another. Only for a moment, but it gave her hope. It also made her realize how scared she was of Dooby, and how little she liked his plans for her.

 **ten**

Zoe looked for William. He was sitting by himself by the huge door that led to the Lady Chapel.

"William!"

"Zoe. That poor boy."

"What . . . ? Oh. The Cat. Yes, I know. It was awful. Is he . . . ?"

"Yes," said William.

"But they're coming. His people are going to attack in a few days. Dooby says so."

"Does he?"

"I'm going to get away," she said in a rush. "I know where my boat is, now. I'm going to get out of here, so come with me! They won't be any nicer to us than we've been to them. It'll be no use saying we didn't want them to hurt him. We've got to get out of here."

"I don't want to."

Zoe couldn't believe it.

"What? They won't be taking prisoners, will they? You'll be killed if you stay! Please! Come with me!"

"No," said William again.

Zoe could see he wasn't being difficult; he was just stating a fact.

"Why not?" asked Zoe, desperately.

"I don't want to go anywhere. It doesn't matter if I'm dead, I'm still going to stay here. And if I'm alive, I'm going to try and stop people from doing evil things. When the fight begins I must tell people not to fight. Try and get them to stop. It's wrong. You understand that, don't you?"

"No!" said Zoe, crying. "I don't. They're all as bad as each other, and you won't be able to stop it! They'll kill you, and you're the only good person here."

"That's not true, Zoe. And they're just people. They're not good or bad. It's just that these are bad times, and it makes people do bad things. I want to help them not to."

Zoe didn't say anything. After a while, it was William who spoke.

"There is one thing that's been bothering me, though," he said.

"What?" asked Zoe, urgently. She was desperate to help William understand that he had to leave.

"Well," he said, "you know that man I told you about? The one who stepped in a puddle?"

"Oh. Yes," said Zoe. It was so frustrating talking to William. She knew there was a good person underneath, a sane person, but he kept on drifting off, talking his nonsense.

"Well, I've remembered he was a doctor, see? And I even remember where he went, but I can't remember his name."

"Oh."

"It's really very annoying . . ."

"I'm sorry," said Zoe, "I don't know."

"No?"

"No," said Zoe crossly. She'd had enough of all his nonsense.

"Go west," William said, suddenly.

"What?" Zoe said.

"Go west, Zoe. When you get away. Things are better there than here."

"So why won't you come?"

He ignored her question.

"West. There's a city you should look for. You'll be all right there. It's a magical place, where everyone is happy, and there's none of this . . . this war."

Zoe turned to William.

"I don't believe there is any such place," she said sadly.

"Oh, but there is. Listen to me, Zoe. I know. It's a marvellous place, and you should look for it. And one day, perhaps, when I've finished my work here, I'll go there, too. And then I'll see you there."

"Really?" said Zoe. "You might come? Where is it? How will I get there? What's is called?"

"It's called Golgonooza."

That was it for Zoe. She had thought William was talking sense at last, but it was just more of his nonsense.

"Golgonooza?" she shouted. "What kind of name is that? I've had it with you! I'm trying my best to help you, I want to help you, and all you do is keep burbling out this rubbish!"

William looked hard at Zoe.

"It's not rubbish, Zoe," he said firmly.

"No? All your silly stories about floods and puddles and so on. They're just stories. It's nonsense, all of it!"

"No, it isn't nonsense. It's important."

"Important? It's stupid. That's why they all laugh at you, don't you realize that?"

Zoe wished she hadn't said that, she didn't want to hurt William, just make him understand. But William didn't seem to care.

"I don't care what they think," he said fiercely. "There's no one smart enough to understand here anyway. I thought you might be different, though. Just stories? I thought you might understand how important stories are."

"William, I'm sorry, but it's not important. What's important is surviving. Not getting killed, that's what matters."

"Exactly," said William. "And how do you think people have survived? How do people remember who they are and where they're from? And how do they know what it means to be human, what makes us more than animals? How do they pass these things on to their children? Stories, that's how."

"Oh don't be ridiculous," said Zoe. "We're trying to *avoid* being drowned! And you're telling stories *about* being drowned! That's no help to anyone."

But even as she said it, Zoe knew that somehow William was right.

"What's the point in surviving if you forget how to be human?" said William. "Stories walk the truth into existing."

"More of your nonsense!" Zoe said, but she was less sure of herself now. William's words had begun to work.

She glared at William, waiting for him to speak.

But he didn't, because suddenly a mad ringing of bells hit them where they sat. Zoe tensed, sensing danger.

"What . . . ?" said Zoe.

"It looks like the attack has come sooner than Dooby expected."

"You see!" Zoe shouted at William. "Now how are your stories going to help you survive?"

"They might not help me, but they might help you," William said calmly.

eleven

The mad clanging of bells was coming from way up in the tower that rose from the middle of the cathedral. Shouts and the sounds of people running reached them.

"Attack! We're under attack. Come on!"

"Hand out the weapons!"

"Cats! Dooby, it's the Cats!"

Zoe ran into the cathedral. She was amazed. The same people that had seemed such a mess to her before were now quickly and efficiently organized into an army. Weapons were being passed out, as Spat and Munchkin shouted instructions. Groups of ten or so were running off to guard various doors and passages.

Dooby stood in the middle of it all, satisfied that they were working as he'd taught them to.

He spotted Zoe. She tried to turn, but he grabbed her arm.

"Come with me, Zoe. It'll be all right."

Zoe felt comforted by his calm voice, and hated herself for it. She was even comforted by the painful grip on her arm. It stopped her having to think what to do. But when she thought of what he'd done to the poor Cat she felt sick.

Suddenly, William stood ranting at the top of the choir stalls.

"Ely is almost swallowed up!" he yelled, his eyes wild. "Lincoln and Norwich stand trembling on the brink of Udan-Adan!"

His shouts of nonsense added to the urgency.

"The wheels of Albion are turning, vast and invisible!"

Then he saw Zoe.

"Zoe! I've remembered! Doctor Foster went to Gloucester. Doctor Foster! Go west, Zoe! West!"

Zoe stared at William, but then Dooby rushed up to her.

"Take this!" he said, and thrust an awful looking pikestaff into Zoe's hands. It was literally a museum piece.

"Just shove it at anyone who gets too close, right?"

"No, I don't want it!" she protested.

"If you want to live, you'd better! Come with me!" And with that Dooby grabbed an ancient-looking sword, with a huge curving blade, and ran for the stairs to the tower. He pulled Zoe after him.

Zoe had no choice but to follow, gripping the pike grimly.

"Udan-Adan is a lake not of waters but of spaces!" William went on with his mad shouting; though no one was listening. "On its islands are the mills of Satan . . . but to the west lies Golgonooza; the city of salvation!"

"There they are!" Dooby shouted.

They stood at a window about halfway up the tower of the cathedral. From there they had a clear view of a mob, carrying similarly brutal weapons, heading fast towards them.

"What are you going to do?" asked Zoe, her heart thumping. She'd never been in anything like this in Norwich.

"Just watch! This should be simple enough!" Dooby was incredibly calm. Once again Zoe wondered who he was and where he was from. He was only a little older than she was.

"The Cats are desperate. They've only got a little zit of an island left now. It's higher than here, but there's barely enough room to turn round. One big wave this winter and they're dead. They've tried this many times, but they're weak now."

"Why don't you let them stay here?" asked Zoe.

"Not enough room. Tough, but that's how it is. We've got a few too many here ourselves. Still, this fight should help our numbers drop a bit."

Zoe was horrified at the bluntness of what he said.

Below them, the army of the Cats met the Eels on the green in front of the cathedral.

"Aren't we going to help?" asked Zoe.

"No," said Dooby, "we've got this under control."

It didn't look like it to Zoe. But Dooby turned to her.

"Just watch this," he said.

From behind the Cats, from the same direction in which they'd come, another force of Eels spilled on to the green. Then from inside some old ruined buildings on either side came two more bunches of Eels. The Cats were caught on four sides. There was no hope for them.

Guiltily, Zoe was relieved. She didn't know what she'd do if she was forced to use the terrible weapon in her hands.

They watched the fight take shape.

Zoe backed away from Dooby, wondering if she could escape.

"All be over in five minutes," said Dooby, laughing. "Look, there's William!"

Zoe had been about to hurtle down the tower, but came back to the parapet. She saw William run out and start yelling more nonsense at the people fighting.

"William!" yelled Zoe from the tower. "Be careful!"

There was no way he could hear her above the noise of the fight.

He continued to pour out a stream of nonsense. Zoe hated him for his stupidity. And she hated herself for not making him see the truth.

"William!" Zoe screamed again, but the noise was too great.

He walked right into the heat of the battle.

"William! No!"

She lost sight of him for a moment. Then she saw him lying still on the grass. She went cold.

Suddenly the bells in the tower started to ring again fiercely. Shouts rose from the nave of the cathedral.

"Dooby! Where's Dooby?"

Someone was calling for him from below.

Dooby ran back down the stairs. He pushed Zoe in front of him. Dumbly, she put up no resistance. She could think only of William, not herself. She didn't want to believe what she'd seen. They were at the bottom. Dooby dragged Zoe out into the nave.

Molly ran towards them, yelling.

"Horses! There's Horses coming! Horses from Gogmagog! We're done for!"

twelve

Dooby grabbed Molly, and shook her.

"Nonsense! Get a grip on yourself. What do you mean?"

"It's true, Dooby," cried Molly. "There's Horses. There's lots of them!"

"Where are the Horses? Are you sure?"

Zoe looked at Dooby. For the first time, she saw him begin to panic.

"They've landed on rafts to the east of the island," Molly said. She was wild with fear. Sarah ran up behind her.

"They're coming!" she yelled. "We're done for, Dooby. There's hundreds of them!"

"Get as many men as you can find and go and meet them! Now!" yelled Dooby. Molly and Sarah ran off.

Zoe didn't think they were going to find anyone.

"Damn!" Dooby said quietly.

"So you didn't get everything out of the Cat then?" said Zoe. She felt pleased by this. Dooby was angry.

"We'll have to put our plan into action a bit sooner than I'd hoped. Come on. We're leaving!"

"What?"

"We're finished if we don't! This is completely different; the Horses are strong, and with the Cats as well we don't stand a chance. Do you want to die? Well come on then! To the boat!"

He shoved the point of his sword at her throat. She nodded. She could feel a little blood trickling down her neck.

Then Dooby ran, tugging Zoe along behind him.

They hurtled down the ruins of passages and streets, ducking under and over collapsed buildings. Rounding a corner they met two unarmed men. Without pausing Dooby charged them, swinging his sword in front of him.

"Eels!" he yelled, and the speed of his attack gave the men no chance. They dropped to the ground in a single heap. Dooby ran on. Zoe didn't dare look at the men as she ran round them.

"Horses!" shouted Dooby as he ran. "Who'd have thought they'd team up with Cats? I should have guessed!"

They were at the west side of the island now. Zoe had never made it this far. There, right at the water's edge, was a low wooden shed.

"Right. Here it is," said Dooby.

He fumbled with a chain round his neck. At last he pulled a key out and unlocked the doors.

"Get that engine started!" he shouted, pulling the doors open.

Zoe ran inside the shed, all the time thinking of how to get away from Dooby.

"*Lyca!*" she said. She looked her boat over quickly. Everything seemed okay. There were the oars she'd pulled from the wall of The Six Swans, ages ago now, it seemed. And there was something new; a small outboard motor fixed to the stern.

They dragged the boat into the water, wading up to their knees. Zoe looked at the engine.

She had never used one, but Dad had told her about them. He had even shown her a broken one once. This one looked okay.

"So how does it work?" she said to Dooby.

"What?" he screamed. "Don't you know?"

"It's your engine!" she yelled back, "I thought you . . ."

"NO!" shouted Dooby. Zoe could see he was beginning to panic.

"I think you pull this cord . . ." Zoe said.

She pulled the starter. Nothing. She pulled again. Nothing.

"It has got petrol in it, hasn't it?" but as Zoe asked the question, she knew the answer. She had never used petrol herself, but Dad had said that it was what made engines work. The blank look on Dooby's face said it all.

"What's petrol?" he asked.

"Oh great," said Zoe. "Well, we'll just have to row for it then."

Zoe fumbled with the crude clamps that were holding the motor to Lyca's stern.

"What are you doing?" Dooby shouted at her.

"It's no use without petrol! It won't go. I'm taking it off. It'll only slow us down."

The useless engine splashed into the water behind the boat.

"Dooby!" A voice yelled at them from the island. "What's going on?"

They turned to see Spat and Munchkin coming after them.

"You were going to go without us! You . . . !" screamed Spat.

"So what?" said Dooby, and turned to meet them with his sword. His usual calm had returned.

Spat and Dooby fought, Munchkin hung back, hesitating. Seeing the fight, Zoe took her chance and put out to sea in the boat. Dooby was having more trouble with Spat than he'd had with the two Horses. Spat was armed with a sword very similar to Dooby's. They splashed wildly in the shallows, thrashing about with their weapons. Munchkin stood nervously at the water's edge, as if trying to decide what to do. Rowing away from the awful fight, Zoe had a perfect view of it all. Suddenly Munchkin jumped into the sea, and started to swim for Zoe's boat.

"Wait," he spluttered. "Take me with you!"

Distracted by this, Spat and Dooby paused in their struggle for a second. Then Dooby snapped out of it. He shoved his sword into Spat. Spat slid into the shallows, which reddened around him.

By now Munchkin was well out to sea, about halfway from the shore to the boat.

"Come back here!" yelled Dooby from the shore. "Come back. You traitor! You're supposed to be taking me!"

Dooby looked stupid, jumping up and down in the water, yelling his head off.

"Munchkin! I order you to come back! Now!"

Munchkin kept on splashing through the water.

Zoe stopped.

"Oh, William," she said. "Should I come back for you, just in case?"

She shipped her oars, and waited for Munchkin to reach her.

After a minute more of splashing, Munchkin grabbed the gunwale of the boat. Zoe wondered why Dooby hadn't tried to follow. They weren't that far off shore yet.

"Come round to the stern. Give me your hand!" said Zoe, and she helped Munchkin over the back of the boat.

Munchkin fell spluttering into the bottom of the boat.

"Take the other oar," said Zoe. "Let's get out of here, before Dooby comes after us."

Munchkin climbed beside Zoe and started to row.

"He won't do that."

"How can you be sure?" asked Zoe.

"He can't swim," said Munchkin, grinning.

"I think he's going to have to learn."

As they rowed away, they could vaguely hear the sounds of the fighting outside the cathedral coming to an end. Dooby was by now a tiny figure standing motionless on the shore.

"Why did you wait for me?" asked Munchkin.

"I don't know . . . I didn't think you stood much chance if I left you to Dooby. And you didn't tell him about what I said. About where my boat was."

"No," said Munchkin, simply. "But what about him? Who do you think won the battle?"

"Who knows? But I think Dooby will be all right. People like him always are. It's William I'm worried about. I wanted to take him with me. I saw him go down in the fight. But maybe he's okay."

Munchkin shrugged.

"Don't be sad," he said. "He would never have left, anyway."

They rowed in silence for a while. Zoe realized they ought to take stock of their direction before they went too much further. She fished in her pocket for her compass.

"Oh no," she said.

"What?" asked Munchkin.

"My compass. I've lost it. It must have fallen out of my pocket when we ran out to the boat."

"So how do we know where we're going?" asked Munchkin.

"We don't. Not exactly. We'll head for where the sun's going to set. That's west, roughly."

"West?" asked Munchkin. "That's what William used to say. Salvation is to the west of the sea. There's a city called Golgonooza. That's what William said, anyway. He was always saying it. It was in one of his stories."

Something clicked in Zoe's mind. She made the connection, and at last understood what William had been trying to say. She felt her heart lift as she thought of him, and of how his story was helping them.

"I didn't think you took any notice of William."

Munchkin shrugged.

"I liked his stories, that's all. Made everything seem better."

Zoe smiled.

"Well," she said, "that's where we're going then."

thirteen

"Zoe?"

"Yes?"

"This is crazy."

"Don't say that."

"But we haven't even got any water."

Munchkin and Zoe were far out to sea. They had watched the island of Eels shrink before their eyes with every pull of the oars. Finally, even the monstrous cathedral had disappeared from view, a dot on the horizon that bobbed into sight for one last time and then was gone.

"Maybe we have," said Zoe. "There's something under the thwart."

They stopped rowing for a while, and pulled the package out. It was a box, wrapped in an old oilskin.

"There you are," said Zoe. "We should have known Dooby would see himself all right."

The lid was stiff, but with cold fingers Munchkin prised it open.

There was a bottle of water, and some dried food in tins.

"What a feast," said Munchkin, smiling.

There was some paper too, folded up.

Munchkin unrolled it; it flapped dangerously in the wind.

It was a map.

"Careful!" said Zoe, grabbing two of its corners.

"It's not as good as mine," said Munchkin.

Zoe glanced at it. Even from the quick look she'd had at Munchkin's map, she could see he was right.

"We can use it, though, can't we," said Munchkin.

"Perhaps . . . If we find some land, then definitely. I just don't know where we are now really . . ."

Munchkin looked at the map again.

"I do," he said. He pointed.

"That's where we are. That's the cathedral, more or less."

Zoe looked.

"So the mainland must be to the west. William was right."

They carefully folded the map back up and put it away.

There was something still in the box. A smaller parcel, wrapped in an old plastic bag. Zoe took it out and unwrapped it.

It was a photograph in a frame. There, in the picture, were three people; two adults standing either side of a young boy, about five or six. The boy's parents had their arms around each other, and around him. All three smiled at the camera. Suddenly, Zoe realized who she was looking at. Despite his age in the photo, the boy was Dooby. The good looks, the dark hair, were unmistakable. It was only the innocent smile that had stopped Zoe from recognizing him sooner.

"Look," said Zoe, and showed the picture to Munchkin. For some reason she felt like crying.

Munchkin looked at the picture.

"That's what it's done," he said, after a moment. "The

sea, I mean. That's what it's taken away from all of us. Dooby, too."

Zoe didn't say anything. In spite of everything he'd done, Zoe couldn't hate Dooby completely. Munchkin was right, they had all had to grow up very fast, and something had been taken from them. Looking at Dooby's photograph, she wondered if, like herself, he was just a child who wanted his mum and dad back.

After they had eaten a little of the dried food, and had some water, they rowed on.

"Where did you learn to row?" she asked him, after a while.

"I don't know. I just watched what you were doing."

"You must learn fast."

"Everyone does, though. I mean, if you want to survive."

"Yes, you're right," said Zoe. She wondered if she could trust him.

"How about a song?"

"What?" said Zoe, between pulls on her oar.

"A song. To keep us going."

"Okay, then. You first," said Zoe, amazed, and trying not to laugh.

Munchkin thought for a moment.

"Okay," he said, "Here's one.

> Little Tee-Wee,
> He went to sea,
> In an open boat.
> And while afloat,
> the little boat bended.
> And that is why,

> my song is ended.
> If the boat'd been stronger,
> my song would've been longer."

He finished, pleased with himself.

"Munchkin," said Zoe.

"What?"

"Let's not sing any more. Okay?"

Still they rowed on. The sea had been kind to them so far, but it was beginning to get rougher. Night wasn't far away, and Zoe could feel the fear welling up in her throat again, as it had the last time she'd set off in *Lyca*.

At least, she thought, I'm not alone, this time. Between pulls she peered sideways at Munchkin. If he was going to do her in, he could have shoved her overboard by now.

"What are you thinking?" she asked him.

"I was thinking about Rat," he said.

"Oh dear!" said Zoe, "He'll be stuck in that little cage."

"No. I let him out when the attack started. I always do. Did. In case anything happened. You know . . ."

"Oh," said Zoe. "Well, I'm sure he'll be okay."

"Yes?"

"Yes," said Zoe.

"Shall we swap sides?" said Munchkin. "My arm's aching."

Zoe laughed.

"Good idea," she said.

"What are you laughing at?" said Munchkin.

"Nothing."

"What?"

"It's just," she wondered how to put it, "it's just . . . you.

You're like a different person since we left the island. You've said more since we got into *Lyca* than I heard you say during the whole time I was there."

Munchkin frowned at her.

"Let's swap places," he said.

Gingerly they swapped places on the thwart. As she stood to let Munchkin slide past her, she suddenly felt how precarious they were, bobbing around on the ocean.

"Aren't you scared?" she asked Munchkin, suddenly, as she slid back beside him.

"No," he said, "William told us where to go. And you know what you're doing. I know you'll get us there. So I'm not scared."

"Oh, right," said Zoe quietly.

They rowed on, and night came. They took it in turns to try and get some rest while the other one rowed, but the sea was starting to happen. The wind was pushing them hard in the face. Zoe didn't like to tell Munchkin, but she had no idea where they were going now.

Soon it was no use one of them rowing alone. Anyway, it was too rough to sleep, so they both grimly gripped their oars and tried to put them into the water properly.

"Munchkin!" shouted Zoe above the wind.

"What?"

"I . . . I don't know where we're going any more. We're probably off course!"

"We can't hold it against this."

For the first time, a wave broke over the side of the boat.

"I'll row!" shouted Zoe. "You bale us out."

She shoved Dooby's box, now empty, into Munchkin's hands. He looked at her blankly.

"The water! Get it out of the boat!"

Munchkin started to scoop the water back into the sea, but before he had made any difference, another wave swamped them.

"Oh God! Oh God! Oh God!" said Zoe.

Munchkin kept baling, but it seemed hopeless.

"Leave it!" shouted Zoe. "Help me point her into the waves."

For a little while longer, they struggled to keep *Lyca* on course, with her nose into the oncoming waves.

Then it ended. Munchkin fumbled his stroke into the water so badly that he went flying backwards. The oar slipped from his hands and was eaten up by the waves.

"No!" yelled Zoe, but she was too late.

Munchkin had leant forward again, grasping for his oar. The boat had turned and a huge wave slammed into their side. Munchkin went flying overboard.

"Munchkin!" she screamed, and without thinking flung herself to his side of the boat. The sea pushed her in after him.

For a second or two she was under the water, then her head broke surface. She gulped for some air. Something pulled at her. Turning, she found Munchkin beside her in the water.

"Zoe!"

He grinned. They grabbed each other for a second, then broke to tread water.

"What now?" he yelled.

"Where's the boat?"

Munchkin nodded. Zoe turned to see *Lyca* a long way off, overturned. The sea pushed her around like driftwood.

"Come on!" Zoe yelled. They tried to swim for *Lyca*.

The waves broke roughly over them all the time now. And

after each one a stinging salty spray whipped their faces, making it hard to see.

Zoe could feel herself tiring. The water was freezing, stopping her arms and legs from working. She went under. She broke surface to see Munchkin a little way ahead of her, still fighting the waves.

She went under again. Longer this time. Strangely, it was much quieter under the water. She no longer felt the cold. She no longer felt anything. Darkness was all around her. She knew she was about to drown. Another second and it would be over. The waves pulled themselves to pieces above her. She tried to look up through the water, and thought she saw a light. She wondered vaguely if dawn was coming. Had they been struggling with the sea for so long? It seemed to be getting brighter every second.

Then with a shock, Zoe thought she felt the bottom with her feet. She looked up again. The light was a brilliant point in front of her now. And then she felt herself being pulled up out of the water. She was being taken towards the light. Pulled upwards by an unstoppable force.

Her head broke through the water and she gasped for air, choking on sea water, but breathing again.

A strong light shone into Zoe's eyes.

"She'll be okay," said a voice.

"Bit close for comfort."

"Yeah. Any more in there?"

"No, don't think so. Let's get home."

The light flicked over her face once more, and she blacked out.

As she went, she just had time to realize something. The light. The light was from a torch. An electric torch.

after

 one

"Hello?"

"Give her time, she'll be all right."

"Hello. Hello? Can you hear me?"

Zoe opened her eyes.

Two women were standing over her, peering at her.

"There, see!" said one of them. "You're all right, dear. You're safe now."

Zoe noticed she was in a bed. A proper bed. Not exactly clean, but like nothing on Eels Island. She was in a white room, with a single window that let in fierce bright sunlight. She thought she could hear the sea somewhere not far off.

She sat up.

"Where . . ."

". . . am I?" The older of the two women laughed gently.

"That's what they all say," the other one said. "You're safe now, dear. I'm Rosie, this is Mary."

Rosie waited for Zoe to say something. She didn't.

"What's your name, dear?" Rosie asked.

"Zoe," Zoe said blankly. She was having trouble remembering everything.

"Don't worry, Zoe. You're all right, now."

"But what happened?"

"Some of our fishermen found you. You were half-drowned. Found you in the shallows three nights ago. You've been very lucky."

Zoe was still confused. She tried to think, to remember, but her thoughts came slowly and then only with a lot of effort. But she was somewhere safe, with kind people looking after her. Bits and pieces started to come back into her mind.

"Is this Golgonooza?" she asked.

Rosie and Mary looked at each other. Zoe saw Rosie raise an eyebrow ever so slightly.

"Never heard of it, love," Mary said brightly. "This is Hope. It's a bit west of what used to be Cambridge."

"But William said . . ." she stopped. The thought of William made her think of someone else.

"Munchkin? Did they find . . . is Munchkin all right?"

"Munchkin?" asked Rosie.

"That boy. You know," said Mary to Rosie. Then turning back to Zoe, "Such a funny name. Yes, he's fine, love. He's been asking after you every five minutes. He is your friend, isn't he?"

Zoe thought for a moment.

"Yes," she said. "He's my friend."

Rosie left to tell the doctor that Zoe was awake. When she returned, she brought the doctor, a huge man with a serious face, but she brought someone else, too.

"Munchkin! Look at you."

He shuffled in behind the huge doctor, looking smaller than ever, but dressed in some new clothes. He looked ridiculous, somehow.

"Are you all right?" he asked.

Zoe nodded.

"She's only just all right," interrupted the doctor. "Beats me why she isn't dead. Both of you come to that."

Munchkin shrank back, but sat himself on the end of the bed, quietly.

"Where have you come from?" asked the doctor as he examined Zoe.

"Norwich," said Zoe.

"Norwich!"

He looked amazed.

"You're either very lucky, or very clever. Probably both. We've had no one come in from Norwich since the last rescue ship."

Zoe's heart immediately started at this.

"They must have been on that ship!"

"Who?"

"My parents . . . I'm looking for my parents . . . they came off Norwich on the last ship . . ."

"I think you must be confused, Zoe. That was nearly a year ago."

"No, you don't understand. They *were* on that boat. They must've been. Black. Rob and Cathy Black. Have you heard of them?"

All three said nothing. The doctor shook his head.

"I'm sorry."

"But you must have!" said Zoe. "My mum was ill. She would have been in here. You must have treated her!"

"Don't upset yourself, dear," said Rosie.

"No listen . . ."

"Zoe," said the doctor, "try to understand. When that last boat came in, things were really bad. We're better organized now. We try and keep a record of everyone passing through. There's lots of people looking for people, you know . . . but it was a bad time. A lot of disease and . . . there was just too much chaos to cope with."

"So they could have been on the boat, then!" said Zoe, her hopes rising again. "Just because you don't remember them doesn't mean they weren't here."

"Yes, but . . . Zoe, you should know. That ship, they had a terrible journey. Lots of them didn't make it. There was a lot of disease. They had to stop at some little island . . . what I'm saying is, don't hope too much."

Zoe ignored him.

"But the people who did make it, where are they? Are they here?"

"No. We were too full here. I'm afraid I don't know where they went."

Zoe had to ask him something.

"Isn't there somewhere called Golgonooza around here? Have you heard of a place called that?"

The doctor gave her the same blank look that Rosie and Mary had. Zoe's heart sank; she had wanted to believe everything William had told her.

"Everyone who came in off that last boat went up to Newhome . . . more houses there, you see," said Rosie, trying to be helpful. "My Billy took them up in his cart. He did ten trips, there and back."

"That's enough for now, Zoe. You need to rest."

"No! I want to go to Newhome . . . I've got to . . ."

"Not now, Zoe."

"Listen to the doctor, dear."

"We'll talk about it tomorrow."

They left, ushering Munchkin out with them.

Zoe stared at the window, too weak to protest any more. She sank back into the soft, soft pillow and went to sleep, dreaming of the sea.

A little while later, Zoe was disturbed by a scratching at her window. It sounded like a rat scrabbling around outside. Then a small hand appeared and pushed the window wide open. It was followed by an arm, and the arm was followed by the rest of Munchkin.

"Munchkin!" laughed Zoe.

"They wouldn't let me in."

He smiled.

"I'm glad you didn't take any notice."

He smiled some more.

"So are we going then?" he asked.

"What? Where?"

"To this Newhome place. To find your parents."

Zoe looked at Munchkin.

"I . . . don't know," she said at last.

"What?"

"The doctor's right. They're probably . . ." she couldn't say it, but Munchkin understood.

"But you don't know that," he said.

"No. But it's like Sarah and Molly said, isn't it?" said Zoe bitterly.

"Don't take any notice of them."

"Well, why else didn't they come and get me?" Zoe yelled at Munchkin.

"Shh! They'll throw me out if . . ."

"It just doesn't make any sense any other way," Zoe said angrily, but she kept her voice down. "They said we were found by fishermen. Fishing means boats, right?"

"Yes, but . . ."

"So if they've got boats here, why didn't they use one to come and find me?"

"Zoe, they've only got two little boats here. I've been asking around. They need them for fishing all the time, or there wouldn't be enough to feed everyone. They don't let anyone use them for anything else."

"They'd have found a way, if they'd been here," she said.

Munchkin didn't say anything for a long time. Finally, when he was sure Zoe was ready to hear what he was saying, he spoke,

"Zoe, how can you ever be happy until you know for sure? One way or the other, you must find out. You've come all this way, you can't give up now."

Zoe was silent. Munchkin could see a tear rolling down her face. Then she looked up.

"But I don't even know where Newhome is."

"I do," Munchkin said, grinning. "I've been asking around. It's further up the coast."

Zoe sighed.

"What would I do without you?" she said, her face brightening.

Munchkin shrugged.

"Let's get going," he said. "They won't let you out for days."

"How do you know?" asked Zoe.

"I've been asking around."

Zoe laughed.

"Listen, Munchkin, you don't have to come," she said.

"I've got nowhere else to go," said Munchkin, "but anyway. I want to."

two

Zoe followed Munchkin out of the window. Once outside Munchkin rummaged underneath a nearby bush. He pulled out a sack. He had clearly been busy.

"Food. Clothes," he said.

Zoe frowned at him.

"We'll pay them back when we can," he said. "Come on, quickly, before they notice you've gone."

He held out some clothes to Zoe. She'd found her old clothes at the foot of her bed, but now she quickly stripped them off and slid into the dress Munchkin had got for her. She looked down at herself.

"Couldn't you have found something a bit more practical?" she asked.

"I didn't have much choice," he said. "Anyway, you look nice."

He grinned sheepishly.

"Well, it's a warm day," said Zoe. "Come on, then."

Now they were outside, Zoe could see Hope clearly. The

hospital she'd been in wasn't really a hospital. It was a large old house, its original owner presumably long gone. The rest of Hope was just bits and pieces. A few real houses, but lots of temporary buildings, sheds and shacks.

There, away to their right, was the sea. It was a beautiful sight. The sun was shining and the waters were calm. It looked so perfect, so friendly, Zoe found it hard to believe it had been her enemy for so long. It had nearly killed her.

"This way," said Munchkin. "That track."

He pointed. Zoe saw a rough path heading away up the coast.

"So how far is it to Newhome?"

Munchkin looked a little embarrassed.

"I don't know," he said. "They were getting suspicious," he added, defensively.

"Doesn't really matter, I suppose."

They began to walk, leaving the small shanty town, Hope, behind them.

As they went, Munchkin told Zoe all he'd found out. Things were better than Munchkin had ever dreamed possible.

"It may not exactly be Golgonooza, but it's not bad," he said. "People are trying to make things work, working together. There's no one exactly in charge, but there's no fighting. They just do what needs doing."

"Things must be better here," agreed Zoe, "just having a hospital. Even if it's not a proper one."

"It's the only one around. If your parents had landed anywhere along the coast for forty miles north or south, your mum would've ended up in that hospital, just like you did. There's nowhere else . . ."

Then Munchkin realized what he was saying and stopped. But Zoe hadn't noticed.

"Forty miles?" she asked. "How much is forty miles? That's so big."

"It's unbelievable," Munchkin agreed, "the island was just a speck of mud. The difference! Look at all this land. It goes on for ever."

Zoe looked inland. Munchkin was right. There was lots of lovely dry land as far as the eye could see.

"But not just that," Munchkin went on, "life's better here. People doing things right, you know?"

"We can't even be that far from Eels Island. We weren't at sea for long enough."

Suddenly Munchkin looked worried.

"What's wrong?" Zoe asked.

"Do you think . . . I mean, if it's not that far . . . supposing Dooby survived, supposing he got here . . ."

Before her eyes, Zoe saw Munchkin start to shrink back, become the frightened mouse she had first met.

"He won't. Even if he made it out of that scrap . . . he'd never find us."

But the thought was enough to make them both quiet for a long time.

For the rest of that day they walked along the rough track that followed the coast, always in earshot of the sea. They saw no one.

For Zoe and Munchkin, it was like a different world. To be able to walk in one direction all day without walking into the sea was a new and strange experience. And with every corner they rounded their amazement grew. There was no end to it; just rolling hills stretching to meet the blue sky at the horizon. Zoe started to love the land.

Still they walked and still they saw no one.

"I suppose most people have moved as far inland as they can get," she said.

"That's what I was thinking," said Munchkin. "Why is Hope there at all? It must be dangerous there, and if the sea keeps on rising . . ."

"I know. I suppose there's the fishing, though."

"It's getting dark," said Munchkin. "We'd better find somewhere to sleep."

"I thought we might get there today . . . it didn't sound that far."

The thought of spending a night in the open made Zoe feel nervous, in spite of all she'd been through. But Munchkin didn't seem bothered.

"We'll find somewhere, a bit of shelter, in case it rains. It's not going to be too cold, anyway . . ."

Dusk was falling fast, and by the time they found an old barn to sleep in, night had come. There was enough light from the stars to find their way in, but once inside they could see nothing. They huddled together just inside the doorway, and slept.

Zoe woke before Munchkin. Bad dreams had gnawed at her all night. She wanted to forget them as quickly as possible, but she sat, still propped up next to Munchkin while he kept on sleeping. Gingerly she shifted a leg that had gone numb. She felt blood begin to bring it back to life.

Zoe's thoughts drifted, but her mind was still as numb as her leg had been. She felt neither fear, nor hope. Neither pain, nor love. She felt empty, that was all. But she felt Munchkin's breathing beside her, and she knew she was alive, at least.

Finally Munchkin stirred. Zoe quickly moved away.

"Don't," said Munchkin.

"How long have you been awake?" Zoe demanded.

Munchkin grinned.

Zoe turned round, and then she screamed.

"Oh! Munchkin! Look!" she yelled, wildly. She turned back to Munchkin, and pointed behind her to the far side of the barn.

"What's . . . oh God! Is it . . . he . . . dead?"

Zoe didn't say anything. The answer was obvious. The old man's body had clearly been shut away in the forgotten barn for a very long time.

"Come on. Let's go."

They left the barn, and stood for a moment, blinking against the sunshine of another beautiful day.

"He must have died in there, sheltering just like we were . . ."

"I wonder who he was?"

"Just someone else, looking for someone, or something . . . come on, let's go. It's too horrible."

Zoe tried not to make the connection, but she couldn't help thinking about William. Was he still lying on the grass in front of the cathedral where he had fallen? She hoped someone had done something for him.

With surprise she found herself wondering about Dooby, too. Where might he be now? Lying in the mud somewhere? He'd been like a king on the island. What he said was what people did. He was the only law. Zoe wondered how he would have managed here – on the mainland. Would he still have been a leader, or would he have been happy just to be alive and safe? But really, it didn't matter to her now. She hoped she never saw him again, and though she knew she could never forget him entirely, she could try and put him to the back of her mind.

With William it was different. She would remember him as long as she lived, because she wanted to.

By midday they had finished their food.

"Couldn't you have pinched some more?" asked Zoe.

"I thought we'd be there by now," Munchkin said. "I didn't know there could *be* so much land. Anyway, I didn't think you approved."

"Oh, I don't know. I suppose I spent all my time on Norwich stealing things. Just because their owners had left them behind didn't make them mine. It seemed worse stealing from the hospital, that's all."

"But that's what they're for."

"What?"

"To look after people."

"I don't think that's what they had in mind."

"There's nothing here to even steal from."

Munchkin was right. They were sitting on a slight rise in the coastline that showed them the countryside around for many miles. There wasn't a building in sight, just miles of fields that had once been carefully tended by farmers, but which now lay overgrown and hidden.

"Why aren't there more people here?" Zoe asked.

"What do you mean?"

"Well, if the country got smaller when the sea rose, then there ought to be more people squashed into what's left."

"I don't know," Munchkin said. He shrugged. "Perhaps they wanted to get well away from the sea."

Zoe nodded. She could understand that, but there was lots

of farming land going to waste here. Maybe there were fewer people than she thought.

"At least on Norwich I could have gone scavenging for some tins."

They walked on and the day moved on with them.

They were beginning to get used to the land now, but only slowly. They had both known nothing but islands all their lives, and it would take a little time before the mainland felt normal to them. For much of the time they walked in silence. Zoe watched Munchkin, deep in his own thoughts. She wanted to know what he would do now, but she didn't dare ask him. Anyway, she barely knew herself what she intended to do. Supposing they got to this place and there was no trace of her parents, what then? At least, they should get away from this part of the coast. Just in case Dooby found them, even though Zoe knew that was very unlikely.

They walked and walked until their legs ached and their feet were sore. There was no sign of Newhome.

"I think William was wrong," she said.

Munchkin stopped walking and looked at her.

"What do you mean?"

"This isn't salvation, it's nothing."

"I know it's taking longer than we thought, but we'll find it."

"I don't just mean Newhome, I mean all of it. What is there for us here?"

"You're wrong," Munchkin said, "it's much better here. There's people organizing things. The nurse at the hospital was telling me all about it. She said the country had been in a real mess, but that things were getting done now. She said in a few years things would be back to normal. William was right. Things are getting better."

Zoe didn't speak.

"Just think about that awful island. I'm glad I'm here. Aren't you?"

Zoe nodded.

"I just wish William was here too."

She walked on, and Munchkin followed.

Then, late that afternoon, a town appeared from nowhere. Coming out of a little gully, they walked up over a ridge and there it was in front of them.

There was a piece of board hammered to a stake by the side of the road. On it someone had carefully handpainted a single word. Newhome.

Munchkin turned to Zoe.

"Well?" he said.

"It's even smaller than the last place," said Zoe after a while. It was the same story again. A handful of proper houses in what had once been a tiny hamlet, but with the same mad assortment of shacks and lean-tos thrown up alongside them.

"Quiet, isn't it?" said Munchkin, then, "look. There's someone we can ask."

He pointed across to the largest of the houses, where a woman had just come out of the door. She was carrying a bucket, and started to hobble across to an old well.

"Come on," said Munchkin, but Zoe hung back. "What's wrong?" he asked.

Zoe didn't reply. She couldn't explain.

"Quick! She'll be gone in a minute."

Munchkin grabbed Zoe's wrist and tugged her after him.

"Hello!" he called.

The woman stopped and waited for them to reach her.

"Yes?" she said.

"Is this where the people from Norwich came?" Munchkin asked.

The woman frowned. Zoe hovered uneasily behind Munchkin. She wished he'd shut up, but she didn't want to stop him.

"That's right," she snapped. "What of it? Anyway, I've got things to do."

She started to walk away.

"No, wait! Please," Munchkin pleaded. "This is my friend Zoe. Zoe Black. She's looking for her parents. We think they might have come here."

The woman stopped, and glared at Zoe.

"Black? Black."

Then she turned to leave, but as she was going she stuck a finger out. It pointed to a small cottage that seemed to cling to the big house for support.

"You'd better go in there," the woman grunted as she hobbled off.

Zoe knocked at the cottage door, after much persuasion from Munchkin. He hung back behind her, and watched as Zoe's knuckles struck the feeble wood. Almost as soon as her last knock had died away, the door swung open. Zoe looked up at the man who had opened it.

It was her dad.

They went inside. Then Zoe just stood. She felt numb. She had tried not to think about what might have happened to her parents. It was too painful. But sometimes, when she needed a little hope, she had allowed herself to imagine finding them. In her mind's eye she had seen this meeting several times. She would rush into their arms, they would all be crying and laughing. But now Zoe just stood, feeling nothing. Munchkin, who had slipped in behind Zoe, tried to hide himself. He hung back in a corner, but it was a small room and even he couldn't disappear in it.

Zoe stared at her parents. Her dad was standing where she had shoved him when he had tried to hug her. Her mum was sitting in a makeshift bed by the side wall of the cottage.

"Why didn't you come?" Zoe said quietly.

"Zoe, darling, we tried . . ." her mum began.

Her dad reached for her, but Zoe backed away.

"Why didn't you come?" she said again, louder this time. Anger rose in her.

"Zoe, Mum wasn't well," said her dad.

"I know, but that was ages ago!" Zoe yelled. "Why didn't you come?"

"Zoe . . ."

"WHY?" Zoe shouted again. She trembled.

"Mum was ill for a long time . . . we couldn't get a boat . . . then . . ."

"Are you still ill now?" Zoe said. She spoke a little more calmly, but she still shook with rage. Her mother didn't look ill. She looked better than Zoe could ever remember.

"Rob, just show her," said her mum anxiously. Her dad looked at her mum with a question in his eyes, and she nodded hard.

"Go on," she said.

Zoe didn't understand what she meant. She watched as her father moved around behind the bed. For the first time Zoe noticed a small cardboard box sitting on a high table. Her father lifted the box down, carefully, so carefully, as though it was made of glass, not cardboard. Zoe stared, struggling to comprehend. Gently, her father put the box down at the foot of the bed. Zoe looked at her father, who pointed into the box.

There, lying on some of the cleanest, whitest sheets Zoe had ever seen, was a tiny creature. Zoe gazed at its little hands and its tiny fingernails. She stared at its little crop of fluffy black hair, at its minute ears, at its beautiful, calm, sleeping face. She looked up at her parents, but just for a second.

"Oh . . . what . . ." Zoe began, but she couldn't speak. She looked at the baby again.

"He's a him," said her dad, daring a slight smile.

"Your baby brother. Zoe, I'm so sorry, but there was nothing . . ."

"Mum's quite old to have a baby. By the time we knew she was pregnant we couldn't risk coming to get you. She was really ill. Then he came early and we didn't get down to the hospital in Hope. It was touch and go . . ."

But Zoe wasn't listening. Tears were streaming down her face. One of them splashed on to the baby's tiny face, and he moved a hand a fraction, but he kept on sleeping.

"He's so . . ." but she still couldn't find the words. Her mum got out of bed and put her arms around Zoe.

"Do you like him?"

Zoe nodded, biting her lip.

"You don't hate him for stopping us from finding you?"

"Oh no!" she said. "He's lovely!"

"I was so worried about you . . ."

"How did you get here, Zoe?" asked her father.

"I . . . rowed, and I . . . I ended up on an island, and . . ." Zoe broke off, staring at the baby again. He snuffled slightly, but still kept on sleeping.

"It was terrible," Zoe went on. "You went there. Mum's pendant. That island. I got stuck there and . . ."

"That awful place!" said her dad. "My God! We didn't dare go ashore. The people, they were like animals, we could tell that from the boat."

"Animals . . ." Zoe echoed.

Munchkin shuffled uncomfortably.

"Oh no, I mean," said Zoe, turning to Munchkin. "Not you. The others, they were all like animals, all except you and . . ."

"Well, don't worry, Zoe," her mum said. "Things are better here."

Zoe turned back to her mum to speak, but her dad got there first.

"That's right," he said, "They may have been wild animals on that awful island, but it's different here. At least people have remembered what it means to be human."

Her father's words reminded Zoe of something she had heard someone else say, not very long ago.

"That's what William said," she said.

"William?" asked her mum. "Is that your friend?"

She looked at Munchkin.

"Oh no," Zoe said. "This is Munchkin."

"Munchkin? That's a . . ."

"Yes, Mum," said Zoe, laughing. "He knows it's a funny name."

Munchkin smiled.

"Hello, Munchkin," Zoe's mum said.

He smiled again and mumbled something.

"So who's William?" Zoe's dad asked.

"He helped me. On the island. I wouldn't be here without him. Or Munchkin."

Then suddenly Zoe realized something. She looked at her baby brother.

"What's he called?" she asked.

"Nothing, yet. He's only a week old."

"Mum's still getting better."

"Please," said Zoe, "please, can we call him William?"

Her mum and dad looked at each other, and nodded.

Zoe gazed at Munchkin, at her parents, and at baby William. And as she looked at her family, she realized that it had grown. There were five of them now. Yes, she thought, five.